D1020561

Provided
by

Measure B

which was approved by
the voters in
November, 1998

A MOUTH LIKE YOURS

DANIEL DUANE

FARRAR, STRAUS AND GIROUX / NEW YORK

A
MOUTH
LIKE
YOURS

Farrar, Straus and Giroux
19 Union Square West, New York 10003

Distributed in Canada by Douglas & McIntyre Ltd.
Printed in the United States of America
First edition, 2005

Library of Congress Cataloging-in-Publication Data
Duane, Daniel, 1967–
A mouth like yours / Daniel Duane.— 1st ed.
    p. cm.
ISBN-13: 978-0-374-21732-7
ISBN-10: 0-374-21732-7 (alk. paper)
    1. Young men—Fiction.   2. Graduate students—Fiction.
3. San Francisco (Calif.)—Fiction.   I. Title.

PS3554.U232M68 2005
813'.54—dc22

                                          2005011503

Designed by Jonathan D. Lippincott

www.fsgbooks.com

1 2 3 4 5 6 7 8 9 10

FOR E.W., WITH EVERY BIT OF MY LOVE

A MOUTH LIKE YOURS

I really do think I'm better off, both for having lost Joan Artois and for having loved her in the first place. And when I think about how we met, I don't even feel the old queasy embarrassment, for getting so out of control; I feel instead a kind of private warmth, an almost visceral gratitude for the changes she put me through, and for the fun we had. Although I didn't know it at the time, I was a complete stranger to myself, and Joan, in addition to being a good time, had an almost pathological compulsion to rip people out of obsolete skins and force them to grow new ones—largely because she needed to do the same for herself and could not. But she certainly did it for me. I'd just come off another heartbreak at the time, and moved to San Francisco alone, after growing up and going to both college and graduate school across the bay in Berkeley. At the late age of twenty-eight, I was struggling with my first adult dating—by which I mean trying not to plunge into commitment with the first person I slept with—and I was finally getting distance from my folks and the scene of my childhood. I was also confronting what almost every grad student does, sooner or later, which is that landing a tenure-track professorship is going to take years of low-paying adjunct work in faraway places, if it happens at all. I didn't think of myself as a failure, since everybody knew a Ph.D. who drove a taxi, or at least the rumor that somebody else knew such a person. But it's awful to be the good apprentice throughout your twenties, earning high marks and fashioning a professorial persona, while your peers go to law school and get married, and then to see it all come to nothing. A sickening vertigo overtakes people, and even while you grow punch-drunk with possibility, wondering what you'll become next, you also wonder how many other bad choices you've made, and how many other falls you can expect to take in life. Or at least I did. But I was also like that—prone to anxiety, and to doomsday thinking, and to crushing self-doubt, despite my happy vanity and soaring enthusiasm. And right about the time I met Joan, I was consumed by the feeling that the movie of my life had run out of money mid-production, and that I was wandering through neighboring studios and envying all the well-funded features in progress.

Partly in reaction, I'd rented an apartment by Ocean Beach, nearly an hour from the U.C. campus, out where Golden Gate Park meets the sea and schoolchildren play soccer and the old Dutch windmill looms tattered above the Monterey pines. I was still teaching twice a week, but I thought the proximity to surf would be soothing—I'd been a surfer since I first got my driver's license and started crossing the Bay Bridge for waves. And like a Rip Van Winkle who's been sleeping too long in the library, I also had this notion that I should somehow prepare myself for the rest of my life by moving to a proper metropolis and finding out how normal adults live. Berkeley's such a comfortable place that people who grow up there often stay, getting ever more ferocious in their good health and their cooking techniques, and campus life is even more insular. All of a sudden I wanted out. I wanted to live in a real city and not fall in love for a while, lift my head up out of the sand and look around. And that's why when the phone woke me up one Sunday morning,

and it was my lawyer friend Bernie inviting me over for pancakes—this is how I'm saying it all started, with Joan—I jumped
out of bed and pulled on jeans and ran through the rain to my
van and drove down the Great Highway, a cloudburst beating
on the van's roof and on the milky-green sea.

Bernie had just bought a house in a quaint and upscale
neighborhood of well-restored Victorians, and while he doesn't
figure prominently in the rest of this story, his wife did intro-
duce me to Joan, and he also had a lot to do with the way I was
thinking about love. Short, wiry, and quick to laugh, with
wide brown eyes and a cropped mop of brown hair, Bernie grew
up in a caring and affluent Democratic home in Shaker Heights,
Ohio. His mother was a circuit court judge, his father was an orthopedist, and he had a quick intelligence and a teasing sense of
humor. With none of my yearning for intensity, or for a "higher
life," he'd made quick work of Stanford Law School and was already ascending the ladder at the U.S. Attorney's Office, where
he prosecuted big RICO cases. The one, single department in
which Bernie had ever been uneven was romance. He gave lip
service to loyal and chivalrous monogamy—which I honestly
thought was my own modus operandi—but Bernie had this tendency to let each three-year relationship bleed six months into
the next. Partly, I think, it had to do with his falling in love less
with what mattered, like decency and compatibility, than with
his vision of the perfect woman. They were always Kennedy
School–Peace Corps types, running off to join Médicins Sans
Frontières in Burma or to do a Ford Foundation fellowship in
Cameroon. And he was such a patient person that he'd always
sent devoted e-mails to some hand-cranked village computer
and even made the difficult in-country trek for a torrid reunion.
But as much as he loved all the high-achieving drama, he also
needed stability, and he had this tendency, after a year or two of
long-distance misery, to fall for the interesting woman closer at

hand. He somehow never managed to tell CIA Susie about Marilyn in Malawi, and because CIA Susie was no dummy, she always found out, and the overlap always poisoned their love from the start.

I used to make a lot of noise about Bernie's amorous unhappiness, because our friendship, like most, had a competitive streak and he had executed every other aspect of life with greater success than I. Berkeley in the 1970s endures even now as a cliché of a libertine town in libertine times, and my own childhood, although sheltered by good parents, had involved an earlier-than-usual start on sex and drugs; by the time I got to college, I thought of myself as having been around the block. For years after graduation, Bernie continued to tolerate this, but then, when we were both about twenty-seven, he decided to apply his big brain to his love life, and everything changed. "No more heartbreak," he declared, after his first-ever split-up without a girl in the wings. "I can't take it anymore, Harp. We *have* to be more deliberate about mate selection." Because he was tired of my playing the expert, Bernie said forcefully what he'd only muttered in the past: that my own romantic record, marred by obsession with what he called "high-maintenance nut jobs," really did not recommend me as an expert on healthy relationships, no matter what I said to the contrary. And I was so porous, just then, that I heard him loud and clear. I wasn't ready to concede that I should do anything differently—my "high-maintenance nut jobs" had also been sexy and interesting, and weren't we all just drawn to whomever we were drawn to? Was there really anything we could do about it, other than continue to seek the One? But I did watch carefully while Bernie dated around, comparison shopping and avoiding entanglement. It was a new approach, in our mutual reality, and it was impressive. He managed to sleep with several attractive women over the space of six months, being honest and forthright and leaving only minor bad feelings behind. Still unsure of what he was looking for, he read a book on evolutionary psychology and learned that humans evolved not to be happy but simply to reproduce. He decided that our problem lay with the very concept of the perfect woman, deriving as it did from the ingrained "search images" by which we all unconsciously choose partners—the spectral composites of our mothers, our cultural biases, and our early childhood memories. Shaped mostly by familiarity, and not by what our hearts really needed, these "search images" sent men again and again after the wrong women. Our mothers, as he put it, might well be perfect for our fathers, but that didn't make them perfect for us. I hated this kind of talk—what do evolutionary biologists know about the human heart?—but then Bernie met Eliza Bruckmeier, the freckled and bespectacled food editor of a San Francisco magazine and the daughter of socially prominent academics. Although every bit as fit and wiry as Bernie himself, she was nothing like Bernie's mother, and she wasn't a poverty lawyer or a diplomat, either. She fit none of his usual patterns. And I honestly didn't think Bernie felt that mysterious gut-level certainty right up front. But he swore that such certainty could no longer be trusted, and that he and Eliza had a great thing. "I just like this woman," Bernie told me. "I plain like her. She's a highly cool individual." He liked her laughter, he liked her taste, and he liked the fact that she'd long since finished her bad-boy phase, having dated junkies and idiots throughout her drug-addled twenties. She had a good job, she wanted a family, and she was ready for lasting love. Eliza also knew that my best friend was a great catch, so she waited only a month before raising the possibility of a shared future. Instead of running away, as I suggested, Bernie surprised me yet again: he found a therapist. Not long after, he decided that he, too, was ready for the next stage. I wasn't exactly skeptical, because I liked Eliza, but I was bumping up against a hardwired part of myself, the part that craved high passion. I was scared that I might not be able to copy his act, or that copying it might be a mistake, or that I was somehow built differently. What if I couldn't just *choose* to love someone because I thought she might be good for me? And, yes, the women I truly loved—the ones I flipped over—they usually ended up hating me. But what if the problem lay less with them—"I'm actually *glad* she left me," I'd said after Esther Brukowski, "because she was a lunatic"—than with me? What if I really *could* have the love I dreamed about, as soon as I finished this long-overdue phase of growing up?

"No, it turns out it's fine," Bernie replied enigmatically, while fixing his round brown eyes on mine, "to love somebody who loves you back."

Eliza often tried out recipes for the magazine, and her ropy arms were flipping orange-ricotta pancakes that morning, on their new Wolf range, and also frying applewood-smoked bacon in their new All-Clad pan and baking a spinach-Gorgonzola frittata. Sitting in their breakfast nook, with rain on the window, and envying their money and their conventional stability, I put my future in their hands, the way I did with almost everybody back then—asking, in essence, What should I do next? I talked especially about the one woman I was already dating, Shauna Rose, and how she was a great candidate for the long term—brilliant, similar goals and values—but that I'd told her I was unready for commitment. Then our conversation wandered to the bad academic job market and a cute new editor I should meet at Eliza's magazine and a string of road-rage encounters I'd been having. The anxiety of change had caused an upwelling of bile in my inner monologue, with the simplest of setbacks, like lost keys or a dropped gas cap, drawing vulgar outbursts.

And this is just the way things went with Bernie, by the way: he'd ask how I was doing, and I'd talk and talk and talk. Then he'd ask more questions, and I'd tell him more, and I'd feel wonderful and as if I were the center of the universe. Then I'd remember my manners and ask how he was doing. And he was so gracious that he'd brush it off and keep the focus on me, and I could never tell if I was supposed to insist. Watching me talk, Eliza appeared to be thinking about something else, and she sifted through a pile of their wedding photographs—an Indian-summer celebration that had shimmered with the cross-pollination of easy money and good values. Then Eliza held up a snapshot and blurted out, "Here's one: Joan Artois. I think you met her at the reception."

Bernie protested that Joan was on the rebound, and pretty nuts, but Eliza reminded him that rebound was perfect for a guy dating around. Then she handed me the snapshot, pointing to a woman in a yellow dress, with rosy-tan Norwegian skin and sun-streaked brown hair. Joan didn't look familiar, but she was sticking out her food-laden tongue, which made it hard to tell. Looking at the photo, I was reminded mostly of the young Jeanne Moreau in *Jules and Jim*. Much like Truffaut's male friends, about to love and suffer and test themselves at the hands of the glamorous shape-shifter, I thought, *Wow, this girl looks fantastic*. Jules and Jim fall for Moreau because they think she looks like a statue they've declared to be the ideal of female beauty, and the funny thing is that Joan looked no more like Moreau than Moreau looked like that statue. In person, Joan can seem strikingly beautiful—depending on your feelings about her—but cameras almost never catch her magic. Only the occasional candid does her any justice, and then only if she's looking right into the lens. As a result, Joan keeps very few photographs of herself, despite being preoccupied with her own appearance. One of the very few I ever saw was a childhood image in Joan's

New York apartment, showing her at age three or four on a Lake Tahoe dock, next to her brother. "Right before everything bad happened," Joan told me, "before I got so goddamn sideswiped. I was still just an innocent." This was Joan's number-one theme, the mysterious disaster that rendered her forever unlike normal boys and girls. And in my own view, at least on that last night of ours, the photo proved that she'd been born this way: already, the feral physical intensity; already, the child's eyes demanding and inviting, laughing and accusing.

The directions led me to an Italianate limestone villa near Hamlin, the expensive girls' school to which my mother had gone, and I do think I'd always been impressed by the privilege of my mother's upbringing. I remember sitting in my car and looking at the building for a while, and getting a warm glow from the vision of my mother in a little uniform, long ago. I was still smiling when I arrived at Joan's cast-iron gate and found her crossing the rose garden to intercept me. I don't remember what I made of this, but I do know that I assumed Joan had grown up here, or that her folks at least owned the place. Neither was true. Joan had simply hidden out with the Cavanaugh family during her parents' divorce—the Cavanaugh son, Sebastian, was one of Joan's oldest and dearest friends. Ever since college, she'd been staying with the Cavanaughs when she came to town.

She wore black heels that night, a navy pantsuit, and a cream silk blouse, and I found the corporate formality intimidating. Graduate school can do that to you, over the years. I remember Joan's pearl earrings setting off her lovely skin, and her wary eyes being so bloodshot that she had to have been crying or sleeping. She offered a firm work-world handshake, wrapping a big hand around my own—offices, powerful men, deals—and her chestnut hair framed a face that looked vague at first glance, Scandinavian and yet indistinct. "Hi," she said, forcing a professional smile, "I'm Joan Artois." Her straight nose conjured a handsome father.

I said, "Hi, I'm Harper. You know, my mother went to Hamlin? Right over there?"

Joan barely registered this, and she looked annoyed when I got in the van before unlocking her door. "Your name's not Cassius?" she asked, pushing aside the sandy towel on the passenger seat.

"I go by Harper."

She sniffed again, looked around to my damp wetsuit, my surfboard. "Why did Eliza say Cassius, then? Was she kidding?"

"Cassius is my first name. But I don't use it."

"What's wrong with it?"

"Nothing."

"Come on, tell me. I smell issues."

"No issues. Cassius Brown was a black civil rights lawyer. My father worked with him in Georgia, fighting the Klan. I just go by Harper."

Joan looked away, as if to remember her manners.

"What's so funny?"

"Just the way you say 'black civil rights lawyer.' "

"The way I . . . what?"

"Well, it sort of trips off your tongue. 'Fightin' the Klan.' I bet you've knocked out a lot of white girls with that line over the years."

"It's not a line."

"Of course it's a line."

"Why would I lie about a thing like that?"

"Weren't we going to get a drink?"

The Cliff House, on the rocky bluffs of Land's End, was a gaudy old place a few blocks from my new apartment, with ornate ceilings and cracked leather booths, penguin-suited waiters and threadbare carpets. Joan headed for the bathroom as soon as we arrived, and I thought, *"Of course it's a line"? Fuck you, lady. Fightin' the Klan. It's the way my father talks. And it's real. He's for real.* When Joan returned, I did my best to entertain her, pointing out surfers in the falling light, but I had a hard time jibing this inward person with the glamorous extrovert described by Eliza: singing a famous part from *Tosca*, apparently, in a university gala concert of scenes and arias. "There's this amazing moment," Eliza had said, "where Tosca's been soaring in the upper reaches of her soprano—a lot of it's about sexual jealousy—and then she's killing Scarpia to protect the man she loves, and as she drives in the dagger and hits the word 'die' her voice dives to the bottom of her register. It is so hard to find a woman who can sing that role, especially at twenty-one. It's almost unheard of—it was the most overly ambitious choice for Joan—but she's like that, and it is the sexiest part in the world. They even brought in ringers for Cavarodossi and Scarpia, because the director really believed in Joan, and she nailed it. She absolutely nailed it. She was so precocious." Eliza had clearly envied Joan, but the roles were reversed now. Eliza relished telling me about Joan's high school drinking problem, and how she just innocently wonders "why oh why all these older men think I'm seducing them!"

"Like her boss," Bernie said. "And her boss's boss, this guy Gujie."

"Joan has the hardest time seeing that it takes two to tango in these sicko affairs," Eliza said. "Or in anything at all. She reads other people like nobody's business. She just looks at you and bam! She'll tell you exactly what your biggest insecurity is and how you're kidding yourself. Right to your face, too, in no uncertain terms. Like, 'Hey, do you realize how childish you are?' But does Joan see her own complicity in anything, ever? Not ever. Spotless as a lamb. Which is why she gets in these messes, because who can live with that? And don't think I'm saying she's gorgeous, either, because she's not. But she's raw sex on an oyster shell. Men disintegrate around her. And she's so clueless she honestly thought this older European businessman, this idiot French playboy named Gujie, she thought he meant it when he said he loved her. It's her whole white-knight-daddy thing. And what she really needs is a nice American guy, her own age—a guy who can accept the baggage and stand up to her bullshit and give her a nice life."

That's me, I'd thought, *the perfectly normal guy who happens to be a sicko specialist.* I'd been certain I would have a lot to say to her, and that she'd trust me more than she'd trusted anyone in ages, and that I'd then lose control and get my heart broken. But perhaps it would be a good challenge for my new approach. In the face of exactly what unhinged my heart, I'd remain calm and collected. So when Joan returned from the bathroom, at the Cliff House, I tried to get her talking about Bernie and Eliza's wedding. Joan's face tightened as she said that she'd brought a man she'd intended to marry and that her own father had re-married on the same weekend. And now she was single, she said, with a sour face, so why didn't I fill in the blanks? I changed the subject to the Golden Pacific Country Club, where Joan and Eliza first met, and where my mother's father was a member. Al-though I was estranged from my grandfather, and he and my fa-ther couldn't stand to be in the same room, I'd been to the Golden Pacific Club a few times myself, and since moving to San Francisco, I'd found myself talking about it more often. My grandfather was an "awfully prominent man," as my mother liked to say, the founder of an enormous downtown law firm. I wasn't above wanting people to know that. But Joan just left for the bathroom again, and when she returned, she rubbed her eyes and nose and sipped her drink and watched the piano player. Five minutes passed without a word, and we seemed almost in separate rooms. Tapping a finger on her glass, occasionally scrunching her mouth, Joan showed no sign of wanting to leave or be elsewhere, but she refused to let conversation flow, offering only that she'd taken her new little stepsister for a facial that day, to the dismay of her new stepmother. I got the feeling Joan wanted to confess something but was unsure how to do it. And this was my classic intuition, my standard opening: *Look, I know you're in a rough patch, and we've only just met, but I really am happy to listen. Try me.*

As if to deflect attention, Joan asked about my work. So I told her—Ph.D., journalism, everything up for grabs. I'm sure I sounded ridiculous, open to suggestion even from Joan.

She chuckled in my face. "I'm sorry," she said. "It's just . . . it's so weird for me to be on a date." She smiled and shook her head, then resumed staring out to sea. Left almost alone, with an apparent injunction against drawing her out, I tried to decide what she looked like—the high cheekbones and the violet tones of her forehead, a round mouth and an awareness of competence. I thought I could see her mind scrambling to make sense of something, and then she looked around the room for distraction, commenting on a row of Marlon Brando photos. Relieved to have something to say, and wanting to revisit my "fightin' the Klan" remark, in order to explain it away, I told her that early Brando was like scripture to my father—the whole moral grandeur of *On the Waterfront* and *Zapata*, stories of Irish longshoremen and Mexican revolutionaries in great left-wing struggles, common men standing up for justice and landing lovely ladies from wealthy families. Great stuff, in my view. Joan looked at me and laughed again, although not in a way I liked, so I told her that my father really had spent years with the Poverty Program and Legal Aid, and that he and my mother had even dined with Mr. and Mrs. Huey Newton once. Still not getting anywhere, and becoming embarrassed, I nervously drew attention to the nearby John Wayne photos, and I told Joan that my mother's father met Wayne in an officers' club during the Second World War, when Wayne came over to rally the troops. My grandfather was an archconservative, I said, in my regrettably stark terms, a stiff Wasp, while my father was a warmhearted Catholic. Joan appeared truly puzzled as to why I thought she'd be interested, but I liked talking about all this, so I told her how Wayne was doing his Hollywood war hero routine when my grandfather and the other fighter pilots walked out. They meant no disrespect, but the Duke didn't know what he was talking about. I'd studied Westerns as part of my doctoral work, so I asked if Joan had ever seen *The Searchers*, a 1956 John Ford classic about a white girl kidnapped by Indians and then rescued by her uncle, played by John Wayne, who intends to kill her if he thinks Chief Scar has violated her whiteness.

"I guess I have *one* thing to look forward to in life," Joan said, her face softening.

I laughed with her, but I had no idea what she meant, and I wished she would acknowledge all that I'd told her.

I still worked as a teaching assistant back then, running a discussion section of a required freshman course called Race, Class, Gender & Sexuality. I slipped into Monday's lecture thinking about Joan, and what exactly had happened to her, and why my stories hadn't worked for her, but I was also relieved that I didn't have to see her again. And soon enough my attention turned to Dean Reynolds, at the podium. "I was actually straight in my teens," the dean told the class, "just like everyone else in high school, and then in college I was in a white sorority, and suddenly I was everybody's sex counselor. And why? I didn't know any more about sex than they did, so it made me wonder—was it my color? Was it the fact that I dated women? And even nowadays, while I'm living as a straight woman and sharing my white husband's last name, I've found that this life, too, has consequences, like some of my old friends and lovers seeing me as a traitor. But I guess that's why I'm so interested in the relationship between sex and identity and power, and that's what I'm asking you to think about this semester—the way in which you all construct yourselves and others in terms of your sexuality and your economic class and color, and so forth. You may have heard it said that when two people make love, there are always six people present—the two lovers and their four parents. We could probably add all their ex-lovers, too, but let's just say for now that the seventh person is culture. Every different sexual position, if we think about it, has a tacitly understood meaning that derives from our culture's language of power, and when we make love, we speak that language. Every time you nudge a lover from one position to another, whether you're on top or on bottom or 'topping from the bottom,' as they say, like it or not, you're in a dialogue with the economic power relations governing our society."

After a brief faculty meeting with the other teaching assistants, I drove up into the flowery, forested Berkeley Hills. And again, I thought of Joan: *I guess I have* one *thing to look forward to.* It was a funny remark: did she mean getting kidnapped by Indians? Or seeing *The Searchers?*

Shauna's pickup was in her driveway, and her old blue Porsche Roadster—the bubble-shaped kind, gift of her brother when he renounced worldly possessions—sat by the curb. Her cottage, with its cedar-shake shingles and smoking stovepipe, made me think of the cozy, not-impossible dream we tacitly shared—that we'd both teach at some rural liberal arts college, where she'd offer Shakespeare and Chaucer and I'd give the annual Hawthorne and Melville seminar, and we'd read side by side on the porch on weekends, stopping only to watch a bobcat in the woodpile, or to share choice sentences. "You so inspire me," she'd once said. "In the sense of 'give spirit,' but also just 'give breath,' since *spir* has both meanings." Maybe we'd even convert the old barn into a library.

A full-figured Eastern European beauty, with an enviable air of self-knowledge, Shauna was a year ahead of me in the program, her dissertation complete, and she was taking the opposite approach to the job market, refusing to be deterred. Already, she was preparing for interviews at Texas, Michigan, and U. Mass. That particular afternoon was perhaps our tenth together, in a pattern set by Shauna herself, and we exchanged our typical greetings—she said, "Hey, gorgeous"; I replied, "Howdy, li'l darlin' "—and my light spank sent Shauna laughing up the varnished pine ladder to the realm she called "the cloud," all white pillows and picture windows among the eucalyptus trees. Much later, when I muttered something about being "fucked silly," Shauna wondered at my tone. "Obstreperous?" she asked.

"Obstropolous?"

"Is that a word?"

"It's from Mark Twain, I think, out of eighteenth-century Southwestern humor writing."

Our conversations trended this way. Shauna punned once that the fish merchant was a "prawn broker," I called Shauna an "errant punster," and then she figured out that I thought knights-errant were either wayward or on errands for their kings when, in fact—as she explained—the term was "arrant," a medieval variant meaning wayward but also unmitigated, thoroughgoing. Ever since, her eyes full of adoration and curiosity, she'd been running a concordance on me. "Pantheon," she might say, "that's your third time using that word in as many days." Or: "Tautology—that's twice in twenty-four hours."

Nodding meaningfully now, Shauna searched my eyes— perhaps suspecting another imperfect usage. ("Have you ever even seen a Fellini film?" she'd once asked, gently, when I called something Felliniesque. "Ah . . . I think so," I'd replied. "Well, maybe not.") Then Shauna cut to intimate matters, asking to hear more about the way I'd been raised—a kind of dream childhood, as far as she could tell. Happy as ever to discuss it, I told her, too, about my father and Cassius Brown and the Klan and my father's one-man law practice, and how my rich and powerful grandfather was a right-wing asshole, and my gorgeous mom had left a life of privilege for one of passion and meaning, although she still loved her father and thought he admired me and saw me as his proper heir and wished her husband weren't so determined to hate the old guy. But I felt Joan listening in, snickering and telling me I was full of shit, and I hated her for it, because it wasn't fair, and because it was making me wonder if I should think less of Shauna for enjoying the story in the way that other people had enjoyed it. I told Shauna about my teething in our Haight-Ashbury flat, too, with drag whores downstairs and a black-magic cult upstairs, Satan worshippers tiptoeing quietly to Midnight Mass as per my mother's request, with the baby Harper sleeping and all. It was one of my mother's favorite memories, and Shauna saw it perfectly. She was a wonderful listener, in truth, often catching unintended mythological or Shakespearean references. Once, when I apologized for going on and on, she insisted that she was getting the whole picture in an instant mental video, as if my language went directly to what she called her "cerebral imaging center," without delay. So I told her about riding a stroller through the great antiwar protests, and how my mother had gotten herself arrested protesting nukes at Lawrence Livermore Laboratory, and how when Vietnamese boat people fled the Communist regime, everyone felt sorry for them, but my mother actually made the phone call: first, a black-and-white photo arrived from a Cambodian refugee camp, and then my mother drove down to Edwards Air Force Base to greet a terrified couple and their three children, none wearing shoes and all their belongings in a single grocery bag, speaking not a word of English.

"You've really never felt beautiful?" Shauna asked, eyes dripping into my own.

"What?"

"I can see that. You feel handsome, but not beautiful."

I took in my own nudity: pink skin, bony limbs.

"I love this fair skin."

"Really?"

"So smooth."

"You mean that?"

"Mm." She shook her head. "And these young surfer muscles. I'm too lucky." She kissed me and said, "You make me downright oozy. It's very confusing."

"Wow, because I've never seen it like that, but . . ."

"Male beauty is so undervalued."

I thought of a boy I'd seen at the beach, and I described the way he'd peeled his wetsuit to the waist, reached up to gulp orange juice—stomach muscle sheet dropping below his navel, the distinct wings of his deltoids. "He was such an Apollo," I said. "A young war god. And hey, what about you? Tell me about your family."

Shauna looked at me funny and reached for a photo album,

and while she hid certain pages and showed me collages of little-girl photos and undergraduate apartments, I decided that her look had had to do with the word "Apollo." So I asked.

"Apollo is indeed a beautiful young boy," she told me, "but not a war god. You had the idea, though." She turned the album to a picture of a lush garden in a forest, with a stream trickling through and . . . a naked body in the water? Shauna herself, in a patch of sunshine? I laughed at her guilelessness and Shauna said, "That's not guilelessness! That's openness, Harper! I'm not trying to hide anything from you." She swore she'd only wanted to show the cabin in the background, but that if I wanted to see nudes, she had plenty: black-and-whites taken by one of the professional photographers whose work she displayed in her bathroom. Body parts, breasts and arms, legs and neck. All Shauna's. She turned next to her mother in a bikini in 1962, looking like a lean young Elizabeth Taylor. On the facing page, for purposes of comparison, Shauna had taped a photo she'd intentionally staged of herself in a nearly identical bikini, at the same age and in the same posture, also walking wet from the waves. It was hilarious, and Shauna knew as much, but the physical similarity was striking.

"Mom's actually shorter than me now," Shauna said. "She's really shrinking. She's not at all the virago she once was."

"Remind me what 'virago' means."

"Well, *vir* is manly, so it's like manly woman. But she's just a dumpling now, a sweet, sixty-year-old dumpling dating the most physically repulsive man. I do not get what she sees in this guy, especially after my father."

Sitting up, I rubbed my face and looked out the window—evening shadows in the eucalyptus, a leaf-strewn slope.

"And off he goes."

I smiled, got one foot onto the loft ladder. I had to be careful now, draw a line. Preserve my freedom to go through whatever I was supposed to go through in my life.

"Eat something first," she said. "And answer a question." While I stepped to her cottage floor and she padded after me, Shauna said, "So, really—are you sure this isn't just becoming your bordello?"

"How's that?"

Shauna's refrigerator carried a bumper sticker from the Bloodroot Collective Restaurant saying *Vegetarians Taste Better*, a handwritten note with the words "Our Bodies Are Our Gardens, Our Wills Are Our Gardeners," and a picture of Bert, Ernie, and Big Bird riding a roller coaster. She brought out a homemade blackberry pie and set it on the butcher-block counter. "Well, I don't know," she said, cutting me a slice, "it's a little weird how quickly—postcoital—you reach cognitive lucidity again. I feel like my own intellectual capacities just disintegrate."

Shauna liked to watch me eat—confessing once, while I devoured a cheeseburger, that it "makes me feel like a real woman with a real man." A family thing, she thought, the way her mother equated love with food. Now she asked, "Do you know the term 'heteroglossia'? From Bakhtin?"

"Ah . . ."

"Well, *glossia* is 'tongues,' so it's really 'other tongues,' but I'm thinking more of Plato's Athens and how women were slaves, basically, at the bottom of the heap, while the men were the philosopher kings. But there was this whole other class of women, of sex workers, called the *hetaerae*—have you ever read Durrell's *Justine*? You haven't? Oh my God. Just a sec." She scampered across the bare cottage floor, took a paperback from a shelf. "Here," she said, "there's this great line where the narrator says . . . hold on. Where the hell is it? You have *got* to read this book, by the way. It's totally *outré* in feminist circles, but it's so sexy. Oh, wait, here, here. Okay. 'The true whore is man's real darling—like Justine; she alone has the capacity to wound men. But of course our friend is only a shallow twentieth-century reproduction of the great Hetaerae of the past, the type to which she belongs without knowing it.' Anyway, in classical culture they were on a higher status level than the wives. It was where the misunderstood politicians and poets and artists would go for solace, and many of these women were self-educated philosophers and poets in their own right, kind of philosopher-whores, though I hate that word 'whore.' Anyway, I kind of feel that way with you—on the divan, musing, you know?"

Slicing more of that pie, I marveled at Shauna's playful brain inhabiting such an earthy vessel, with its asthmatic lungs and strong shoulders, and at her willingness to hold nothing back, to volunteer the self.

"See, it's so great that you recognize that," Shauna replied. "It's a strange ride, being me. But look, I'm just asking myself, you know, what *roles* are available to me. I don't know quite who I *am* with you. I mean, you come here, we make love, and you leave, and then you come back. And I'm not complaining. I'm a lucky girl. But I also wonder, you know, am I some woman out in the prairies, thinking, 'Okay, it's springtime, and those ranchers ought to be coming through sometime soon with them cattle—I sure hope that handsome one's with them! Oh goodness! Here they come! I better get the pancakes ready!' I mean, I'm starting to *feel* that way with you! It's like, whose story am I living?"

I knew exactly what she meant, but I could not yield ground. This was the crux of the matter.

"For example," she said, "don't you have a birthday soon?"

"Wednesday."

"And how old, again? You've told me, but I think I blocked it."

I said that I would be twenty-nine, and Shauna buried her face against my shoulder. "God, we are almost exactly the same age. Would it be presumptuous to offer you a birthday dinner? I don't want to overreach."

Joan, unfortunately, called me the next morning. I was crossing the Bay Bridge at the time, and she was very calm and detached, asking only if I would meet her at a beach in the Marin Headlands. She said it was her very last day in town, so I agreed. I had to park at a dirt turnout at the edge of a cliff and then pick my way down a steep trail to the bay channel. Walking up a strand of smooth black pebbles, I found Joan sunbathing on a towel, wearing a two-piece brown swimsuit and tortoiseshell sunglasses that conjured a teak Kris-Kraft. As soon as I sat down, I sensed an optimistic expectancy, as if she were only a visitor in this world, about to return to the far better one she missed. She seemed eager to kill time, and she was fixated on watching the seagulls and sailboats. I was equally fixated on not being the chatterbox I'd been at the Cliff House, so for over an hour we made stilted small talk and she watched every tack of a white yacht on the blue water. The Golden Gate Bridge soared overhead like an airborne luxury liner, and cormorants and grebes glided along the shallows. The Seacliff mansions, over on the San Francisco side, dangled Babylonian gardens.

Joan's long hands lit a cigarette and then put it out. Then she lit another and said, "I'm glad I'm finally leaving, but I do wonder sometimes why I don't live out here." This appeared to be more than a passing thought, as if moving home was a real possibility. "Why do I always think I have to be so far away?"

She let the sun onto her face and for a long time she barely spoke at all. Another half hour slipped by in silence.

Then Joan exclaimed, "Wow, that skinny guy over there is hung like a horse."

I saw what she meant.

"I wish all my queenie friends were here."

Changing the subject, I asked to hear about her life in New York—just impersonal details, like the nature of her job. And although she had sought me out and invited me here, she actively withheld information, saying only that she worked "for a production company," doing what she called "overseas stuff." I asked where in Manhattan she lived, and Joan said, "God, that's right. I wasn't even thinking about that. I guess I live downtown now." *Oh gee, okay. Well, where in fucking downtown?* "The West Village." Joan fell silent again, apparently with a lot on her mind—her lips even moved, once in a while, with half-muttered thoughts. So I amused myself with the smell of kelp and the feel of the wave-worn driftwood. At last, when I couldn't bear the awkwardness, I said, "Okay, Joan. Come on. A penny for your thoughts."

Her voice was soft and intimate as she said, "Well, I am thinking . . ."

"About?"

"Mmm . . . how to say this? I just should, right?"

"Of course."

"You're as sweet as you seem?" She poured sand from hand to hand, her mouth twitching from smile to annoyance. Then she said, "Okay, own it. I am thinking, Cassius, about touching."

Touching? Not where I thought we were going.

Joan poured sand from hand to hand with the rhythm of the surf, and when she turned to face me, she said, "In fact, I was thinking about touching you."

I glanced away from the fine golden hair on her arms and the bare skin at her hip. "Joan," I asked, "would it be all right if I kissed you?"

She looked surprised, pushed hair out of her eyes.

"It's okay if you don't want to."

She smiled as if the whole concept had come out of left field but wasn't such a bad one. "No, it's fine," she said, brightening. "You can kiss me."

I leaned forward, but Joan stayed where she was. I paused halfway, embarrassed, and she grinned. She said, "Are you going to kiss me or not?"

I put a hand in the hot black sand and Joan watched my approach. She let me remove her sunglasses, but she didn't return the kiss. She pulled back instead, holding my eyes. I hopped a knee closer still, but Joan dodged and smiled at me.

She said, "You're not being sincere."

Hmm?

"You're mocking me."

"No, I'm not."

"I'm afraid you are."

"I am not mocking you." I was irritated now.

"You are. You're playing around, like the big TA."

The tenderness of Joan's self-exposure—and the dexterity with which it vanished—were mesmerizing. I moved forward again.

She said, "Not until you play nice."

I had no idea what was happening.

"Come on, Cassius."

"I go by Harper, not Cassius."

"But just kiss me, okay? And be with me? And don't jerk me around?"

I wanted dearly to do both. "How am I jerking you around?"

"Because you're acting like this is a game."

"I am?" I had no idea.

She nodded with certainty, her tenderness replaced by arch awareness.

"Okay, sorry. Look, I was just . . . I don't know. Meet me in the middle, okay?"

"No chance."

I swallowed. "Why not?"

"That's your job. You asked to kiss me."

I took a breath and blinked my eyes and rose yet again to my knees. Moving toward Joan in all sincerity, I finally made it to her lips, and she kissed back, and we lingered in the big surprise of two mouths that somehow got along vastly better than their corresponding hearts. While time slipped by in the sunshine, and that kiss went on and on, I started to wish things were different. I started to wish we could sleep together someday, and that I wasn't dating someone else, and that we could tease out all the similarities in our Bay Area childhoods. Maybe I'd even fly to New York for a weekend. I traced her breastbone with a finger and we settled into the sand, easing closer.

But then, without warning, Joan jumped to her feet and stood over me and said, "I have to pee. Turn around."

Dumbfounded, I looked out to sea and heard shuffling noises. I noticed a cold south wind and I slowed my breathing so as not to be overeager, and then Joan said, "Hey, let's go, huh?" I whipped around to find her stepping into her blue canvas sneakers. Her mood had flipped; she seemed angry and miserable, and I wanted to reach out and kiss her again, but she wouldn't look me in the eye. Her voice testy now, she said, "You coming or not?" Then Joan bundled her belongings and walked off, sand still clinging to her thighs.

Watching her go, I bit my tongue and wished I knew how

to put her at ease. Sun burned my neck and a container ship emerged from the glare, HYUNDAI in giant letters on its side.

Back at her borrowed BMW, which was parked beside my van, Joan had already pulled on her flower-printed white jeans and her white sleeveless blouse, and she sat in the driver's seat. I tried to tell myself what I knew to be true: that it didn't matter what I'd done wrong because I'd done nothing wrong. I told myself that whatever she thought I'd done wrong, I'd been around enough to recognize an unstable personality when I saw one. But I also couldn't see any reason not to ask what the hell she *thought* I'd done wrong, because I hated wondering if maybe she wasn't half-crazy at all and I was in fact a horrible guy in some way I couldn't quite see because I was a fucking shit-head.

"What do you mean?" she replied, a vein swelling on her forehead. "Really, what does that mean?"

There had to be a way to turn this around. "Joan," I replied, "I just mean that we were having a sweet kiss and then . . . a wall came up."

"A wall."

"Yeah."

"God, you're a chump."

"I guess I'm not putting it the right way, I just really, really do not want to part on bad terms with you, and I . . ."

She shivered slightly. "There's no wall."

Please don't shut me out. It's like my worst thing. "Because, I don't know, I . . ."

"Look, we had a nice time, okay, young man? And now we're done having a nice time. And fortunately, we never have to see each other again. So you can keep all this bullshit to yourself, right? And let me go on my merry way?" With a curt little wave, Joan drove off and left me wondering if Joan was a lunatic, I was an asshole, or I was an asshole lunatic.

Sitting in the Econoline, I tried calling Joan's cell. She didn't answer, so I drove toward the bridge. Before the on-ramp, I called again. This time Joan answered and said, "What do you want?"

"Let me buy you a drink."

"Are you kidding? I told you I have to pack."

"Where are you?"

"Why do you think you can just call me?"

"Come on, pick a place. I'll buy you an early dinner. You can pack later."

I heard a chuckle. "You're incredible."

"Are you meeting somebody else?"

"How could that possibly be your business?"

Please please please. "Name a bar. Anywhere."

"Where did you learn to behave like this?"

A silver Camaro roared onto the bridge, a bald man at the wheel.

Joan gave me instructions to a Marina District tavern, and while I pulled the van into traffic, I called Shauna and, unfortunately, made up some self-justifying baloney about why I needed to reschedule.

Post-Greek singles gathered outside the Balboa Café, in a once-unpretentious old fishing district cleaned up for the getting and spending of premarriage professionals. A slender man with fashionable eyeglasses walked out of the bar, climbed into a tan Range Rover, and jostled the white Cherokee parked in front. Nudging the red Honda Civic behind, and then retapping the Cherokee, he drove away. I took the spot and marched into the Balboa Café's old-fashioned room—just the right wood floors, plaster walls, and black-and-white photos for a timeless

American watering hole. Joan already sat at the bar, and she asked, "So, what do you want?"

"Okay, look. I feel terrible."

"You do."

"I do."

"Well, that's nice. So then what the hell *was* all that?"

"Which part?"

"While you were kissing me."

"See, I'm genuinely sorry about that, I . . ."

"Were you attracted to me, Cassius?"

I asked if she was kidding.

"Do I sound like I'm kidding?"

"Well, of course I was attracted to you, Joan. Honestly. Calm down. I mean, I still am. You're a very beautiful woman."

"How are you attracted to me?"

Was this a joke?

"Come on. In what way are you attracted to me?"

"You really want me to count the ways? Okay, you seem very intelligent, and very much your own person, and . . ."

"Keep going."

"I don't know, you're very articulate, and I get the sense that . . ."

"That's all very noble. Do you want to fuck me?"

"What?"

"Do you want to fuck me or not? Look, when I said I was thinking about touching . . ." She fumbled for cigarettes. "I can't believe I have to explain this to you. What exactly did you think I was saying?"

That she was thinking about touching?

"All I meant was that we'd *already* touched each other, okay? Figuratively speaking. And I was thinking about how it happened. You made me laugh so much at the Cliff House, and the best part was that you didn't even know it. You weren't even trying, you were just being yourself. And I knew I should've been alone on my last day. I regretted inviting you as soon as you got there, because I could tell you had some childish frat-boy fantasy about the forward woman."

I'd made her laugh?

"I didn't come here to make up with you, Cassius. All I'm saying is that you put me at ease, which is very rare. And for two people who only just met, something special and sweet happened, and I wanted to honor it, okay? And now I just wish we'd managed a one-night stand before I started hating you."

I grabbed the back of Joan's neck and yanked her mouth to mine. I had never done anything even vaguely like this, but Joan giggled with surprise and kissed back. Then she pulled me into a corner of the room, leaned into the wall, and held me against her while she laughed. Kissing me again, she said, "Holy moly, Opie." She shook her head. "Way to go. Very nice." As if playing an old and delightful game, she muttered, "Now say something dirty."

"What?"

"I want you to say something dirty."

"Like what?"

"Whatever. Anything."

Dirty. I recover from the kiss fiasco and already I'm off balance again. But I refused to fail. So what came to mind? *Blow me, bitch? I want to fuck you with my big cock?* Clearly unsuitable. "Well," I said, "I'd like . . ."

"No, come on, really." She took one of my belt loops in each hand and tugged. "Be genuine."

"Okay, then," I said, struggling, wondering why this wasn't so easy, "I have been wanting to take off your jeans, and . . ."

"No, no, no."

"No?"

"No, come on. You've got it in you, I can tell. Just say what you're thinking."

Turn the tables. Do something. "Why don't you tell me what you want to hear."

"Why is this so troublesome for you?"

"Okay, give me a sec. I'll try again."

When Joan saw that I was lost, her laugh rippled like a spasm. "Hey, don't strain yourself," she said, falling into a looser hug. "Maybe this isn't your thing."

But what kind of a guy would that make me? "No wait," I said, at a complete loss, "how's this? I'd love to suck your pussy."

Joan's jaw fell open and her eyes glazed over. "That," she said, her face tearing into a grin, "is absolutely gross."

In a final effort to hang on, I said, "Well, then, why don't we go back to your place?"

"Because I have to pack! I told you that."

"Come on."

We stopped first for burgers, and then I followed Joan to the Cavanaugh mansion. She told me not to park on her block, so I found a suitable spot and then jogged up the street and through that tremendous garden. The big door had a complicated lock—it took Joan several tries—but we emerged at last into a grand, silent home, all the inhabitants away. We left our shoes by a bench in the entry hall, and Joan led me up mahogany stairs and down a hall of closed doors. In a corner room, high windows caught the last of the pink sunset on the dark bay, elaborate crown molding surrounded the ceiling, and a white bed occupied the middle of a polished-plank floor. Muttering something about her own foolishness—"I cannot *believe* what a bad girl I am"—Joan pulled back a comforter and turned over the sheets. While she undressed, she told me to turn off the light. "I don't look very good without my clothes," she said.

"That's not true."

"I'm afraid it is."

Eyes adjusting, I stepped out of my sneakers.

"What are you doing?" Joan asked.

"Taking off my jeans."

"Don't. I know it's weird, but it's better for me that way. Take off your shirt, though."

Once we began to kiss, Joan seemed faintly disappointed by my lead, as if I weren't giving something she knew that I had. "Forget it," she said, with a grin, when I tried to take off her underwear for the third time. "It's not going to happen." She sat up for a sip of water.

I said, "So, are you looking forward to New York?"

"Why do you care so much?"

"I don't."

"I'm not going to New York, Harper. I'm going to prison."

"What?"

"Oh my God, you believed me."

"Well, where are you going?"

"The Amazon."

"Come on."

"I'm telling the truth now."

"You're going to the Amazon."

"I'm meeting a friend."

"Oh."

She stared at me in the darkness, a grin on her face.

"Well, hey. That's great."

"You're too much." She chuckled.

"And your work doesn't mind, huh? All this time off?"

"They're terrified of what I could do to them. But hey,

don't tell anyone about tonight, okay? Like Eliza and Bernie? It's been nice knowing you, but you do seem like a blabber-mouth. And I'm sure they told you some bullshit about me; Eliza's incorrigible that way. I really don't want to find out six months from now that I was fodder in your little local sewing circle."

Nothing happened the way I'm saying it did. But let's try this next, because it gestures at the shape of my life back then.

"Hey, knockout," I said, at Shauna's front door.

"Hey, drag-down."

I saw the pot of soup, the big salad, and I felt immensely relieved. I said, "You're too nice to me."

"I know." She wrapped her arms around my waist. Jade mountains dangled from her olive earlobes. "But come upstairs, anyway," she said. "I need to get up on my perch."

"Your perch?" I had an edge, a little residual frustration over Joan.

"That's you, baby. Mr. Perch."

"Sounds fishy."

There was something unusual about the sheer strength of Shauna's abdomen—high school gymnastics?

"Just born this way. Boys on the soccer team used to take turns standing on my stomach." She called her physique the "deluxe compact model," by contrast to the long-boned woman-of-action she yearned to be.

When I squeezed, she didn't compress. "It's almost emasculating," I confessed.

"No, it's not. It's quite masculating."

"Really?"

"It loves when you squeeze hard, and it definitely yields."

Why did this bother me?

Later, in the falling darkness, her blue eyes round, Shauna spoke up again: "I love how in your body you are."

"Tell me."

"I'm always happiest when I'm in my body, and not just in my mind. You get that from the ocean."

I smiled.

"Hey, what kind of birth control do you prefer?"

What?

"For the long term."

"Ah . . ."

"Because my last boyfriend . . ."

"The actor?"

"Before the actor. He refused to use birth control at all, except for the rhythm method, because I guess he thought diaphragms ruined the spontaneity, and he couldn't feel anything with condoms, and since a woman doesn't ovulate while on the pill, she doesn't have some smell that women get when ovulating and he can't get interested in sex. We couldn't sleep together for about two weeks out of the month—especially the two weeks when I really wanted to. And then I got pregnant. Which is another story, and sort of sad. But, look, I'm just saying that I'm willing to go on the pill. Let me know, though, okay? It takes a while to kick in."

"Hey, Shauna."

"Mm?"

"Ah . . . look. About the long term."

"Mm?"

"You know, right, that I'm not ready for all that."

"Of course."

"I just don't want to end up feeling like a dick."

"A dick?"

"Yeah."

"Ah, my fine old phallocentric friend."

"What?"

"Don't get the wrong idea. I'd be phallocentric, too, if I had such a lovely phallus."

My heart lifted and I looked below. "Really? You mean that?"

Blinking and smiling, Shauna shook her head. "My oh my, you have been so underappreciated, my personal golden dawn, moon lighting the left side of your face and sun lighting the right." Kissing my arm, she said, "Are you aware that I adore your freckles?"

"You do? No. What's to adore?"

She pressed her lips on the inside of my elbow. "I think I've just always dreamed of loving a boy with freckles. And these long, slender limbs!" She ran a finger down my leg. "They're so . . . I don't know . . . *colt*like. I'd love to be built like you."

While she finished cooking, Shauna settled me onto her futon couch. She'd draped a tapestry over the desk and computer, to hide them while not in use. Her cinder-block-and-plank shelves carried stacks of *Semiotexte* and *Renaissance Studies*, and her travel itinerary lay on the coffee table: two days at U.T. Austin, two at Ann Arbor, four in Boston. She'd stop in New York for a week at the end, to visit her mother. Before returning to the stove, Shauna said, "Now don't freak out, okay, but I got you a couple of birthday presents. And I did it purely because I wanted to. No obligation." Then she handed me a fragrant shaving soap that, when I smelled it, made me feel anxious and surly, and a mix tape with "Give Your Love to Me," by Queen Latifah, that made me even more anxious and surly, and a photocopied collection of love poems from Pablo Neruda,

e. e. cummings, John Donne, and the eleventh-century Japanese poet Izumi Shikibu that caused me to fidget and wonder how I could get the hell out of here, and also why on earth I wanted to get the hell out of here, when she was so lovely and kind. Shauna had also included that snapshot of herself naked in the garden stream, back bent over a round rock, water circulating between her legs. Most outrageous of all, she'd included her recipe for blackberry pie (all italics mine):

CRUST: 1 cup flour, 1 stick *softened soy margarine*, 6 tbs. chilled water
FILLING: 4 cups ripe ollalieberries
Fill pie crust with berries, then combine the following ingredients (beat until smooth) in a bowl and pour evenly over the fruit: 1 beaten egg, ⅔ cup melted soy margarine, 1 cup brown sugar, 1 tbs. flour.

I was crazy about Shauna. And in my heart of hearts, I valued openness, unguardedness. But I was desperately trying not to do exactly this—to slip-slide half-blind into yet another year-long commitment that went sour. I needed to reevaluate a little. I needed to grow. And I hated the fact that in the growing I was apparently going to lead somebody on. Somebody I should be thankful just to know. And that hatred turned to guilt, and the guilt turned as always to anger, and soon I was thinking the most ungenerous of thoughts—like that I had already eaten far too many lame-ass vegan desserts in my short life, and that vegan cookies really were heavy, mealy, and bland, holding not a single candle to the basic Tollhouse recipe on the back of twelve million Nestlé chocolate chip bags worldwide. Try it yourself. Buy the chocolate chips. Follow the recipe. Smile. End of story. And this here pie recipe was even more preposterous, I almost muttered aloud, because it called for soy margarine in the crust, and *an egg* in the filling, and veganism required you to eat only plant products. So what was the code? Could it be that butter was the pastry equivalent of the brambled rose? And that we liberal academics couldn't tolerate even the hint that we were complete motherfucking strangers to ourselves?

"Hey, Harp," Shauna said, drifting over from the stove, "what's going on?"

"Can I use the toilet?" Excusing myself, I locked the door and glanced at a black-and-white photograph of a naked woman pouring water from a gourd and another of two naked women leaping through the air. Then I closed the open medicine cabinet on Shauna's aromatherapy bath salts and looked in the mirror: just my face, a little angular, gap-toothed due to my hippie father's unwillingness to spring for orthodontia, crow's-footed blue eyes behind boyishly collegiate wire-rimmed glasses, receding red hair ever uncertain of itself. And then I asked, What Is Really, Actually Happening? Because I'd always been clear with Shauna. I had no moral issue here. I'd been perfectly straight. And yet actions also have meaning, and I was even then standing among the body products and linens of Shauna's deft nest building, the entire cottage a testament to her rich intellectual life, and all these massage oils testament to her truly healthful eros, and I could smell from under the bathroom door the evidence of her willingness to overlook my prickliness and make a birthday dinner. So much about Shauna made sense for the man I was, despite my mother's underhanded disapproval—"I think it's so sweet," she'd said, "that you find Shauna attractive." More confusing still (and enraging, if I'd been able to admit it) was my lovely mother's instinctive sympathy with Joan, who was gone for good and whom Mom had not even met. "It's so nerdy to ask for permission before kissing a woman," Mom had said, when I told her of the day at the beach. "And it's so unnecessary. You're a very sexy man, in that grand leading man way, like

Cary Grant or Gary Cooper. Any woman who's alone with you on a beach is dying to be kissed by you, and she just wants you to come in there and take charge and do it."

Sitting down now, on Shauna's closed toilet, I flipped through her magazine basket: the exact same periodicals I subscribed to, plus *Ms.*, plus a few books, like Susan Sontag's *Against Interpretation*, Thich Nhat Hanh's *Being Peace*, and *Daily Affirmations for Adult Children of Alcoholics*. "Pick one!" I wanted to scream. "You can't be all these different women simultaneously! Articulate a coherent persona!" But of course I was only looking for excuses, rationalizing this impulse to keep her on a string and not drive her away, and perhaps also recoiling from the way she mirrored my own divided self. So I grabbed her *Tao Te Ching* and plunged a finger into my nostril and tried to slow my breathing. "When living by the Tao," Lao Tsu writes, "awareness of self is not required, for in this way of life, the self exists, and is also nonexistent, being conceived of, not as an existentiality, nor as nonexistent." Flipping around, I found more: "The sage does not contrive to find his self, for he knows that all which may be found of it, is that which it manifests to sense and thought, which side by side with self itself, is nought." Not very helpful. I found a back issue of *Ms.* next, and read the following headline: "Hot, Unscripted Sex: How Women Are Redefining Sensuality and Pleasure." Wasn't this the whole point of Bernie's search image theory? Time to grow up? And yet here was the rub: my mother was in fact a great beauty. And a sex kitten. And a fountain of adoration and flattery and supportiveness, despite her certainty that I could be so much stronger, silenter, more financially successful, and despite my having once expressed displeasure with her, perhaps five or six years earlier. "Academia is so wrong for you," my mother had always said, whenever I told her how much I loved my research or enjoyed teaching, "all those weenies backbiting each other over nothing at all. Why not go to law school? You could work with my dad and have a second home in Tahoe and a happy life." And meanwhile, Shauna's *Ms.* magazine had an article called "Eroticizing Equality," telling of a journalist's worry, upon being asked to throw a bachelor party for a friend, about the antiwoman character of the traditional strippers, whores, and straight porn. The journalist hoped to replace the old misogynistic horrors with the benign contortions of gay-male porn and the nobody-gets-their-feelings-hurt innovation of a cross-dressing party theme, as ways of challenging his guests' traditional visions of male heterosexuality—which made my skin crawl. Because this was precisely the lunatic campus sex world I inhabited, and it was also precisely the one I needed to escape. The journalist complained that "feminist men" couldn't get laid without either feeling guilty about the inherently oppressive and sexist nature of hetero sex, "reinforcing patriarchy," or being utterly passive in bed, and although this made me want to berate Shauna for thinking this jackass was setting a great example and that I was, too, that I was her beautifully evolved and feminist California prince, I had to admit this sounded familiar. And because it sounded familiar, I wanted to claw my eyes out in shame. "What I love about you," Shauna had once said, trying to put me at ease, "is that your male and female sides are so well balanced." Now I wanted to strangle her for the kindness. So, back to the journalist, the big pansy, looking dutifully and honorably for a middle ground, trying to assert what he called "a nonoppressive sexuality" toward women (probably even asking for his kisses, instead of grabbing the dame and taking them like Cary Grant) and getting soundly rejected. Because who the hell wants a nonoppressive sexuality?

I'd made a flurry of phone calls over the prior few days—as was my habit, unable to trust my own judgment—in the hopes of generating consensus that Joan was manipulative and bizarre, and therefore just as well gone, despite my preoccupation with her, and despite the mixture of queasy nausea and pride she'd given me. I'd even told my mother everything—as I always did, back then. She never liked hearing about my post-breakup miseries, but new passion was her bread and butter; she loved thinking of me as a successful sexual being, a real Svengali, and she always fished for detail. In response to my story about Joan, however, she offered only the speculation that the Artoises were one of what she called the "old-time San Francisco families." When I pressed Eliza to make me feel better, and tell me what to think, she shared an anecdote about once falling for an ugly man *because* of how masterfully he'd swooped in to kiss her. Bernie, for his part, said, "Joan really asked you to talk dirty to her? That's fantastic! The only time a girl ever said something like that to me, I was so scared I couldn't open my mouth. I just did her as hard as I could. You think that's lame? That's probably lame." Eager to achieve in this department, I'd dropped by A Clean Well-Lighted Place for Books and found *The Fine Art of Erotic Talk*, by Bonnie Gabriel. Taken in by the subtitle—"How to Entice, Excite, and Enchant Your Lover with Words"—I'd turned right to Chapter 8, on "Talking Dirty." A list of suggested sentiments included "You've got a warm heart and a beautiful pussy, and I'm honored that you open both of them to me so completely." Not so useful. Or: "Sir Lancelot would like to pleasure Miss Kitty right now. Do you think she's ready?" Certainly gallant, but how about the following, along the veins of my bumble at the Balboa Café: "I want to make love to the virginal parts of you that no man has ever touched before. I want to lick your pussy like it's the first time. I want you to lick my cock like it's the first time." Hopeless, of course, although it would perhaps do wonders for Shauna, being nonoppressive.

Was that fair to Shauna? No, that was not fair. So, dropping Shauna's magazine, I rubbed my eyes and rummaged further in her toilet-reading basket, picked out an aquamarine copy of Jean-François Lyotard's *The Postmodern Condition*. We'd both studied the book in a required seminar, and I flipped the pages now amid the comingling of lavender and sandalwood smells, thinking again about Bernie's "okay to love somebody who loves you back" remark, and how Shauna was never anything but affectionate. So here was another piece of the puzzle: why the worry that Shauna liked me only because she didn't see me clearly? Why did I always think that the only women who saw me clearly were the ones who knew, at bottom, that I was an asshole and not living up to my potential? Lyotard, to whom I then turned for assistance, demonstrated that Western history up through the middle of the twentieth century was dominated by the great meta-narratives purporting to explain everything, like the forward march of Western Civilization, Marxist historical teleology, and the survival of the fittest. These grand stories had apparently created the illusion of a universal human history, justifying terrible oppression all over the world. (Africans and the Irish, for example, considered earlier on the evolutionary ladder than Europeans, were naturally incapable of self-government.) In the modernist period, in the mid-twentieth century, we'd attempted to replace these clearly bankrupt ideologies with new ones, like the liberating rationalism of technological progress, or the comforts of idealized pre-Christian cultures. In the current, postmodern period, Lyotard argues, we know that life has no universally shared meaning, only contingent delusions and temporary inventions, and also that life has no deeper meaning, that our selves and our "psychologies" are merely empty, shimmering surfaces.

A sudden new rain banged at the cottage roof and I looked around at Shauna's calming body wash and eggplant restorative rinse. Bearing into my right nostril with my right pinky finger, I decided that Lyotard's first notion, about meta-narratives, was the one to integrate. I had promised nothing to Shauna, she'd promised nothing to me, and I felt guilty only because I'd bought into the obsolete meta-narrative of lifelong romance—or so it seemed while I was locked alone in a bathroom and using the ruse of a long predinner powder to breathe deeply and make sure I didn't say something too mean and send Shauna packing. Clearly, this was just another residual luxury of modernism, foisted upon the world by people like my parents who not only still told tales of sudden youthful lust but continued to perform a convincing sketch of hot and heavy marriage, despite my mother's ambivalence about affluence left behind. "You wouldn't believe," Mom had told me, after a cocktail party she attended alone, "the way Susan Tate looked at me when I told her your father was off surfing with his buddies. I could just see her thinking, *My God, he must be so good in bed*." And the truth was, that kind of talk freaked me out even then. I didn't know it, and if you'd asked, I would've said, "Hey, my folks just have a great marriage. Don't knock it, okay?" Because even hinting to my mother that she shouldn't say such things to me was to invite screaming tears and accusation and a falling sky and then a whirlpool of self-loathing on my part for being such a shitty and vindictive person. But in some unacknowledged way, it was already making me uncomfortable. Along with the way she managed to rub a breast against my arm every time she saw me. It never, ever failed. I loved her, I loved her doting on me, I did think that I'd never be happy if I couldn't find a woman equally exciting, but there were also certain things I wished she would keep to herself. And if I was honest with myself, I probably doubted that Susan Tate had thought anything at all about how good my father was in bed. But as far as I knew, this was just what great sexy marriages were like. And Shauna didn't even speak the same language. She liked me, she liked that we were peers, she liked that I laughed at her jokes, and she wanted a long-term partner. Which was all perfectly sane. And I liked her back. I liked having sex with her, and I even loved that stupid blackberry pie, soy margarine and all. Tasted pretty good, truth be told. Even with ginger-tofu ice cream. And I'd be a fool to blow all that. Even if Shauna would almost certainly want to tongue kiss while we were both chewing our first bites of this meal she was making—a weird peccadillo that I should not judge harshly. Standing up now and flushing into the sewer the partially cathartic but purely imaginary crap I had just taken, I decided everybody knew that when it came to love you had to embrace the postmodern condition and know that there were no firm answers or deeper meanings, and think more about finding good company for the next leg of life's train ride than with that train's final destination.

"What?" I asked Shauna, when I emerged from her bathroom. "Why are you looking at me?"

"You're not doing very well, are you?"

"Don't worry about me. I'm fine."

"Do you not want to be here?"

"Of course I want to be here. I'm *determined* to be here, in fact." I hated Shauna's gaze, at moments like this.

"I don't look up to you, Harp. I just see you."

"Right."

"You're so used to sliding around in all your separate spheres, you know? All your different images?" She paused. "Making sure your contexts never meet. The one who thinks he has insight into others."

I had no idea what she was talking about.

"Giving people these various parts and pieces of you, whatever parts you want them to see." Another long pause. "And all I'm asking for is the whole story, Harper. Who you are. I know you're seeing other women, and I know you're going through something in your heart, but I don't know any more than that.

And at some point, I need this to become a two-way street. And you look like you can't even decide if you want to yell at me or cry."

True, but useless information. "Aren't we going to eat dinner?"

"Jesus, Harper. Please tell me what's going on."

"Not a thing. Just hungry, that's all."

She nodded and then sighed. "See, this is why I made my No Graduate Students rule. I should have hung tough."

"No, you shouldn't have."

"You were just so cute in the mailroom that day."

"You were, too. God."

"Won't you spend the night?"

"Of course I will. But why are you asking it like that?"

"I just want us to be together in the morning, for once."

"What difference does it make?"

"It seems like I keep annoying you at the end of the day, and I'm so much better in the mornings, with all my boundaries intact. It's like they break down all day long, and by the time I see you, I'm so squishy I apparently drive you crazy."

"Squishy."

"Are you in therapy?"

"I don't need therapy."

"You should give it a try."

"I do not need therapy, Shauna. That's not my problem."

"I know a great guy."

I couldn't open my mouth.

"Look," she said, "I got another interview, at N.Y.U. . . . ."

"Holy shit."

"I know."

"What did you put in that dissertation?"

"I'll be back East for three weeks. Until the twenty-sixth."

"So long."

"That's what I'm saying. Do you think you'll still want to date me?"

"Why do you keep asking this? Of *course* I'll still want to date you."

"Maybe even meet some friends of mine, when I get back? Or is that pushing it?"

Joan called from San Francisco International Airport. She said she was thrilled that I'd answered the phone. I was equally thrilled. She'd thought of me all the way home on the plane. I'd thought of her the whole time she was gone. She had two days before returning to New York, and she wanted to buy me a drink. I didn't have to be on campus again for almost three days. "Or do you have a girlfriend?" she asked. "I certainly don't want to intrude." Nope. No girlfriend. Around the corner from my apartment, at an unpleasant bar, Joan suddenly wanted to share, and I wanted more than ever to listen. I learned nothing about her mysterious male traveling companion in Peru, and a great deal about how people had always told Joan she could be anything she wanted—an opera singer, a psychiatrist, a CEO. She'd always thought they were wrong. I told her they were right. She felt average at best. "I'm not even very pretty," she said. "And for some reason people always tell me I'm beautiful." I told her she was in fact quite beautiful. With a forced twinkle in her eye, and something frantic in her gestures, she said that she saw this moment as a gift. She was finally getting the courage to become herself—not everyone's expectations of who she could be but the very different woman she'd always kept hidden. I liked the sound of this. The big corporate job, she said, and the "bad-values relationships," these were all so wrong for her. Despite the fact that I wasn't going to get attached, this was music to my ears. A fog was lifting in Joan's life, and soon she'd be able to see again. Soon it would be time to write a screenplay or join the Peace Corps, open a French restaurant or finish her Ph.D.

We made out all night, on the floor of my studio, by the beach. We never made love, but we rolled and kissed and stared into each other's eyes. The next morning, with only twenty-four hours until her flight, we drove up the coast. I still knew perfectly well that she was trouble, but there was also something unusual about our chemistry, and she sounded so hopeful. And I was only dabbling anyway, seeing how far I could go without getting entangled. A lovely woman was willing to spend time with me, and I was going to be strong enough to accept that, and not expect more. This new story of hers, about shaking off a dysfunctional past and seeking a stronger future—it was like catnip for me. Such a will to change! Such confidence that she could drag herself right through the portal of personal growth! So I quashed my jitters and told myself that a single night couldn't hurt. Why not have a good time? In fact, maybe it would be a good test, a way to prove that I could control my heart even when faced with precisely the kind of charismatic histrionic that so pressed my hot-sex-and-total-dependency buttons.

While we drove north on Route 1, Joan's attention varied like the day's wind, blowing its warmth all over me and then all over the world outside the van, and then dying down and leaving us both becalmed, unsure what to say. She talked about her trip, too, and while she still managed to avoid all mention of her fellow traveler, she said how much she'd loved the old colonial hotels and the private plane flying so close to a volcano that she'd seen a mountaineer's footsteps in the snow. I told her I'd climbed some big snowy mountains myself, and that I dreamed of climbing in South America, but she kept right on talking—at some Andean hacienda, the rancher's son, a famous toreador and the most eligible bachelor in Peru, had shown Joan the horns of bulls he'd killed, the jaguar pelt on his waterbed. Seeing her ride a horse, the toreador begged Joan to stay behind. The story was nuts, of course, but this, too, was my kind of nuts. It was so romantic, so embracing of life. The more Joan talked, the more I wished that I'd been along on her trip. She described a big blue butterfly deep in the Amazon, seen under the shamanic influence of a rainforest hallucinogen. "Butterflies are my new totem animal," Joan said. "Starting life as a caterpillar and then going into a chrysalis and growing wings. And hey, Cassius," she said, "tell me something. Where did you get the guts to kiss me that first day? At the beach?"

I laughed.

She mimicked my chuckle in a silly baritone and said, "No, come on, tell me."

Wasn't it obvious?

"Really, what on earth gave you the idea you'd get away with it?"

"You're joking, right?"

"Of course not. I want to know."

"Joan, do you not remember what you said to me? That you were thinking about touching me?"

"So you actually *are* the most conceited man I've ever met." The thought pleased her. "Is that what you blabbed to everybody? That I came onto you at the beach?"

"What else could you have meant?"

"You really thought I wanted you." Disproving this point was intensely important to Joan. "Who did you tell this to?"

"It's none of your business. Are you honestly going to claim there's nothing inviting about 'I'm thinking of touching you'?"

"You probably said, 'She wants me. She cannot resist my

masculine *power*.' Do you realize I didn't like you at all? When you first showed up that evening?"

"Really?"

"I thought you were just one of Bernie's boring lawyer friends. And I still want to know what they said about me."

"You thought I was . . . Really?"

"Yep."

"Well, when did you start liking me, then?"

She laughed.

"Because you did take me home with you, right? And you did call me yesterday morning."

"Okay, I guess there were two things. The first was at the Cliff House. I forget what I said, but you said something like 'Tell me why you think that.' And then you said, 'I mean, I'm sure I can guess, but I'd rather hear you say it.' "

"That was good?"

"That was great. I shivered. But then you said almost the exact same thing a minute later and I was repulsed all over again."

"What was the second thing?"

"Back at the Cavanaughs' place, when we were fooling around. You probably don't even remember this, but you lifted me off the bed at one point. I felt very held."

We stopped for groceries in Point Reyes Station, and despite my insistence that I was on a budget, Joan filled our shopping cart with expensive Australian Shiraz and triple-cream French cheese, cured meats and berries, and mangoes and breads and chocolates. Then, when our cart reached the register, she disappeared to the bathroom, leaving me with the very substantial bill. Afterward, we drove along Tomales Bay, past the oyster farms and little docks. Vacation cottages clustered where a river ran a brown plume into the Pacific, and a few miles north we parked at a small cove. I surfed while Joan walked around tide pools and picked up hermit crabs; later, with the side door open, we lay on my van's sandy mattress. Joan smiled through my kisses and said, "See, this is what I kept remembering about you, in Peru. You're so . . . something. I don't want to bloat your head."

"Oh come on, bloat it."

"You bloat me first. Tell me I'm beautiful."

"You're beyond beautiful."

"Make me believe it."

I sat up on an elbow and kissed her again, and we did make love, but with an awkward anticipatory quality, as if I should lead the way in some articulate ritual I'd never even seen. The pressure overwhelmed me, and after a few minutes, I fell beside her and stared at my van's red ceiling. The windows radiated the dusk.

"You all right?" I asked.

In a sweet pout she said, "I want you to fuck me some more."

Wow, this girl had a mouth.

"Please?"

I kissed down her navel, but her hand appeared in my way.

Hmm?

"No chance."

"Why not?"

She yanked me back up. "Come on," she said. "Just fuck me."

Grinning with embarrassment, I started the van and drove us up the coast to the rancher's gate that lets you into Orbin Hot Springs. Across a mile of private pastureland, I opened another gate into National Forest. Half-remembering a series of mazelike logging roads, I took us to a meadow backed by sequoias overlooking the ocean. Lupine ran among the sprinklings of paintbrush and mustard, and a narrow path led through the skinny second-growth trees to a gurgling creek where locals had built a concrete tub over a geothermal spring. The last of the sun caught bugs over the rushing water and we sank into the hot water, sat on the slick green algae. Cooling on the rim and then soaking again, Joan alluded to "everything starting" in her awful childhood, and she talked about graduate school and living in Europe with a professor named Sigmund, how their relationship imploded when she discovered his real age. New York came next, and that's when she'd met Gujie. "And ever since I've been in California," Joan said, "and down in Peru, I've been realizing that I'm always so wrapped up in whoever's right in front of me that I lead a series of half-lives, in terms of myself. It's my big obsession right now. Like you, you lead such a singular life. It's so coherent. You'll be a professor, and you'll have a nice, quiet career, and I'll hear about it and I'll envy you. Because I'm always so open to everybody that every four or five years I get going on some road I believe in, and before I know it, I'm sidetracked by some man I didn't even choose who makes me believe I'm his dream girl and starts getting big ideas. And then it all unravels. I hit a landmine nobody told me about, and then I'm down with the bottom of my leg blown off and everyone saying, 'Oh gee, look at Joan. She was so promising. She could've been an international diva and now she's living in a trailer.' And that's what I think I'm going to learn how to stop."

I tried to tell Joan that I was on the same page, but she seemed annoyed by the attempt to connect, or threatened by it, as if she needed reassurance that this was her world and I was only a visitor. We'd brought spaghetti and sauce, so I just boiled water and kept my thoughts to myself. Joan, meanwhile, chatted with the other campers: a pair of ranchers' wives on a girls' night away (horoscopes, a little Tarot work); and then a beautiful, sad-eyed Frenchwoman who ran an Oakland homeless shelter. I had a couple of old beach chairs, and for much of our meal, while swatting mosquitoes, Joan continued this odd practice of confessing and sharing without tolerating any sharing in return. She talked at length about her "half-lives" notion, the yearning to know why she never got a solid purchase. "Like Gujie. Two months ago, well . . . let's just say that he was showing me blueprints for a house on Majorca. It sounds like a joke, doesn't it? And with Gujie, it could be. He once hid in my closet for six hours, waiting for me to come home, so he could lunge out and give me a heart attack. But I was all set to move to Grenada with him, and be a mommy and dance the Sevilliana forever after, and then he blew it. And now I'm eating spaghetti in a lawn chair with a graduate student named Cassius."

"Maybe not a grad student for long, though."

"What do you mean?"

"Just don't write me off."

She laughed out loud, right in my face.

"What?"

"Nothing, Cash. You're priceless, that's all. And by the way, I like your first name and I think you should own it. But doesn't that all seem perverse? And I guess I want to know why it keeps happening, like what exactly my parents did so wrong, in my stupid childhood, that I have such bad judgment about men. I mean, did they just get drunk and leave me in the park one day? Or what? I mean, why do I always feel like such a booger on my own finger that I'm constantly trying to flick off? And why is my life at risk of becoming one near-miss after another?"

We made out like teenagers again that night, all searching stares and patient caressing, and Joan's talk was mostly lines from songs and animal sounds, a kind of performance for herself—even quipping in the accent of some unnamed foreign man. "Eess no so much of *seemilar*," she said. "Eess, ah—how you say?—more of . . . *deeferent*." She sang a Joni Mitchell song, too, and I remembered hearing the same song in college while watching Esther Brukowski—who hadn't been entirely unlike Joan—sculpt a nude and lament my unfortunate coldness, the difficulty of ever truly trusting me. This was during one of our many passionate reunions, after a huge fight and then days in which I'd waited sobbing outside her classrooms begging forgiveness for crimes I couldn't even understand, and the Joni Mitchell song was about being selfish, sad, and hard to handle, and having just lost the best baby she ever had. I was reading a Margaret Drabble novel at the time, about a single pregnant woman pining for the married man who knocked her up, life pouring over her like a waterfall—the book reminded me of my mother—and I was still certain that Esther couldn't truly love me because she was all broken up over the prior guy, or maybe it was her father, or something like that, and somehow these voices—Joan, Joni, Drabble, and Esther, and the memory of a girl named Vicky Freelon, in the tenth grade, and our long blur of adolescent experimentation—they all merged now into a chorus singing of the other man everybody loved so much and really ought to forget in order to love me.

"But wait," Joan said, while I slipped her underwear off her ankles, "you can't just have me already. I mean, of course you can. But tell me something first." She was anxious, and eager not to be. She pulled the blue sleeping bag to her chin.

"Like what?" Drops rattled the windshield now.

"A story."

I thought a moment.

"Or anything." Anxiety flickered in her eyes, and she said, "I should not just yield to you because you're smitten."

"What on earth makes you think I'm smitten?"

"You're smitten as a kitten. Which is so pointless."

"Why?"

"Because I don't live here. And you don't live in New York.

And there is no way I can be responsible for another person's feelings right now."

"But I can't either, so we're even."

"Right."

"What do you mean, 'right'?"

"Look, just use me, okay? And don't expect anything? Because I am absolute poison."

"Fine. I'm fine with that."

"And soothe me first. Caress my stomach again, like you did before. That was very nice. And no, not *there*. Just the stomach for now. And . . . well, okay, that feels lovely. But *tell* me something."

I remembered a silly psychological test I'd once heard: "Picture a cube in a vast plane, then describe your relationship to it."

"Ah . . . okay. It is approximately of my own dimensions, and it has mirrors on all sides. But the mirrors don't show me if I look in them."

"Really?" How about that.

"Just came to me. Proceed."

"Now describe a ladder in that same plane."

"A jasmine trellis? Does that count?"

"Now a horse."

"How about a massive black Arabian stallion, and I've got my fist rammed up its ass to my elbow. Oh my God, look at your face." She laughed out loud and said, "Okay, scratch that. You're telling me this is what's wrong with me. Let's say it's standing behind me with its head on my shoulder."

I kissed her breastbone and then her navel, and I said, "Okay, now you're walking through a storm with that horse. Describe the storm, the scene, what you do with your horse."

"A big winter storm? Snow and the whole deal? I guess I gut the fucker with an Excelsior knife and pull out all its goopy entrails and crawl inside. Oh no, you're freaking out again. See, I am so poorly socialized. Okay, here it is: a warm storm on a white beach and we're lying there together, just holding each other."

I loved this girl. She was out of her mind. "And the last part: you get through the storm and see flowers. Describe them."

"Big, strong-shafted roses in the walled garden of a castle."

Liking this image, I parted Joan's knees, but she said, "No way, good-looking, you got to tell me."

"Tell you what?"

"What I'm like! What you know about me now."

"Tell you what you're like?"

"Yeah, now that I've done your cheap little Rorschach. Tell me who I am."

"You're doomed."

"What? No, that's way too scary."

"You are. That's the diagnosis."

"No, come on, tell me. I can't handle that."

"Well, the cube is the way you see yourself."

"I look in the mirror too much."

"Except you can't see yourself."

"That's bad, Cash. That's what I'm like."

"And the ladder's how you see friendship."

"Flowery's nice."

"A little flimsy, though. The trellis? You got to admit that's flimsy."

"That is flimsy."

"And you were right about the horse. It's your life mate, the man who can expect to live with your fist up his ass. And the storm's your journey through life with that mate."

"Where I gut him. See, I do need to change. I'm going to change. Can I change?"

"Of course you can."

"Okay, okay. You can do me. But this is what I'm talking about. I need to change. I need to be a more spiritual person with simpler values. I need to find emotional balance and inner confidence and a beneficent empathy for the weakness of others."

"And how about those roses?"

"Children."

"And what did I say?"

Roses, castle.

"Hey, why are you moving like that?"

"Like what?"

"In circles, or whatever. I sense another woman."

She was right: that thing Shauna liked.

"Just fuck me, okay?" Joan's voice quivered with sudden rage, so I did my best.

She stopped me again, her tone darker still. "You've never heard of sex, have you?" She stared, impatient. "Apparently not. So let me give you a pointer: don't try to please me."

Oh God.

"We barely know each other, and we don't have time to get to know each other, and you apparently don't know how to please a girl without being a manipulative weirdo, anyway. So just fuck me as hard as you can. It's not so bad."

I tried, and lasted only moments.

Afterward, Joan curled into a ball and whispered, "Can I ask you a question?"

"Of course."

"What's the longest time you've ever had sex?"

This woman was unbelievable. "Plenty long," I replied, thinking, *Right? Yes, right. A normal guy.*

"Tell the truth."

"That is the truth. Hours. Days. I'm just nervous with you."

"Don't blame me, Cash."

"I don't mean that. I just mean that I'm nervous. For whatever reason."

"I knew from the moment I met you I could make you come in a minute."

"Bullshit."

"I absolutely knew that." She grinned.

"On the sidewalk in front of your house?"

She bit her bottom lip, smiling. "Yep."

"You looked in my eyes on the street, the first time you saw me, and thought to yourself, *I can make this guy come in a minute?*"

She nodded.

"How can you possibly have known that?"

"I'm a very sexy girl. Roll over." Drawn entirely inside herself, Joan rode me loudly and happily, yellow candlelight warming her neck. Then she fell over and her interest evaporated. I waited for a sign as minutes drifted by, and I thought again of Esther ("It's not what you did wrong, Harper, it's what you didn't do! It's what you *never* do!") and also an OB-GYN nurse, for example, from my first year of graduate school: "I don't love you, Harper. And I'm not going to love you. Can you deal with that? Can we still have sex?" Little Vicky Freelon, too, the very first girl to unglue my heart. Clear back in the tenth grade, she'd been the pale-blue-eyed daughter of a tract-home developer and that one blighted girl in every town, the one about whom, fifteen years later, a guy at the CD bin beside you says, "Oh yeah, I remember you! You were in love with Vicky Freelon! Dude, did you know she blew me and like six of my friends at the Polo Grounds?"

Joan coughed in the patter of the pouring rain, maybe asleep and maybe not, and the sleeping bag fell away from her bare back, so I kissed between her shoulder blades. I even tried to remember what I'd done so right at the Balboa Café—grabbing Joan's neck, the brutal assertiveness. Joan tolerated my lips now, purring through her ribs. I kissed each vertebra, and then she said, "Why can't you let me fall asleep?"

Good question.

"Really. I mean, how many women have you failed to satisfy who then politely let *you* pass out?"

And wasn't this, too, familiar? Not so much with the OB-GYN nurse ("Now wait, you mean actual sex for an hour straight? God, I'd really have to like the person"). Nor with Esther ("I think I'm going to lose my mind a little, and I think there's going to be a lot of sex"). But definitely in the way little Vicky had drawn out the promise of taking my virginity—thirteen lovers already in her own past, at age sixteen, she'd taken me to a seedy urban hot-tub place on the bad part of Polk Street that rented private rooms by the hour without checking I.D. (All these hot tubs!) This was even before the appalling scene in her bed, with her unwitting father in the room, before the fights and the unforgivable things I said: the dull-eyed cashier giving the Room 14 key to the stick-thin boy with the studiously torn jeans and the girl in the plaid skirt and knee socks, both clearly stoned. It was in that sweaty-walled room that I'd taken off my clothes with slow, frightened ceremony and eased down to the tub's submerged bench, probably the tenth couple of the day, and was gradually made to see how little agency I had in the thing. Which was what felt familiar, I supposed now: anticipation, the fear of messing up, my vulnerability in the face of blatant manipulation. The content had been different, of course, all about proving that I really was that one boy she'd been waiting for, the one who truly *could* be trusted, the one with whom the lovemaking would be meaningful and sincere. But my paralysis had been very much the same, as I'd watched Vicky dance us to the brink again and again, touch and retreat and take pleasure from my growing desperation, my attempts to close the deal, and my crippling certainty that if I expressed even the slightest annoyance she would explode with fury and leave me forever. For forty-five minutes she'd kept me convinced that life's great miracle was only seconds away, that she was right on the brink of believing all my promises, and then she'd hopped out of the tub and put on her clothes.

But Joan did not leave, despite the fact that I drove her to the airport, and kissed her beside my van, and breathed the sweet stench of spent jet fuel, and ached for her to go. I loved how thoroughly and carefully she gave herself to a kiss, and I also wanted to duck this bullet. I wanted her to disappear from my life without my having to work up the courage to make her go. But while we stood at the curb, she began to look happy and frightened. She muttered something about California being too beautiful to leave for good. She looked up at white clouds and the green San Mateo hills and worried aloud that her life lay here at home. She was suddenly feeling so much better, she said, and she was afraid that if she stayed in New York she'd sink again. A traffic cop looked at us funny, urging us to move along. A limousine driver honked. Then Joan got back in my van and closed the door and said, with a smile, "If I stay, can we play a lot? And still have you not fall in love?" I nodded, worried for the first time that I really might *not* be able to not fall in love. But I was also flattered and thrilled and wondering if, once again, the challenge wasn't exactly what I needed. "Then drive," she said. "Right now. And don't expect anything from me." I nodded, badly wanting to be capable of not expecting anything.

"I'm serious," she said. "Nothing at all."

"You got it."

And in a sense, it was a dream, as we spent the next two weeks in a blur of kissing in restaurants and copulating in public places, with Shauna gone East and Joan's time still limited. But as the days went by, I seemed to upset Joan with more regularity—as if she sensed that my heart was awfully weak to her, and that my promises were half-empty. It made her anxious, I think, in the way Shauna had made me anxious. And the more anxious she got—indulging in my body and my time and my listening ear, and still refusing to accept a shred of responsibility for my feelings—the more testy she became. Her language also grew more abusive, trending toward such castration vehicles as "pussy," "baby," and "feckless fratboy." She also refused to make any plans in advance: she came and went from my flat at will, with no advance warning, and she snapped at me if I tried to pin down specific times when we might meet; once, when I made the mistake of suggesting we leave town again, she exploded in fury. But Joan also spent hour after hour in my company, whole nights and days without leaving my futon. So I told myself and everyone else who would listen that I was thinking maybe I shouldn't interrogate life so closely; maybe I shouldn't ask so many questions. She was clearly unstable—to this, everyone agreed—and most thought she was so clearly my past type that it was uncanny. I retorted that maybe all the best women were just like this. Maybe passion and rage were flip sides of the same coin. And we weren't getting involved, anyway. We were just dating.

I still didn't know what had happened to Joan in New York, or why Joan's employers were "terrified of what she could do to them," or who the other guy was, but for the moment I was doing my best to breathe deeply and stay calm and focus on not being overly entranced—like when she was feeding a parking meter or drooling on a pillow, midnap, and I was unconsciously studying her every move, as if to solve some mystery in my own life. She insisted on absolute privacy—no double dates, no introductions to friends or family, and a sworn promise to tell nobody a thing about our time together (a promise I was breaking daily). This was a particular obsession of hers, and it flowered strongest after our fights, when she'd demand to know how I was misrepresenting everything to others. But she also made me listen by the hour to her confessions. "Anal expulsive," she told me over mocha-chip ice cream, naked at noon and naming her own psychological type, "creator-destroyer. You know what I used to do when I was a baby? Take poo out of my diapers and ambush people, throw it in their face and laugh. Pretty dark, huh?" I was even intrigued by the way Joan teased me into holding doors, and walking between her and the curb, paying for every meal. I wondered if Gujie had treated her this way, and because I knew she still loved Gujie, I wondered also if this was her vision of a proper man. Perhaps I shouldn't rush to judgment. Perhaps I could learn.

At a prix fixe Berkeley restaurant—run by my former Montessori-school teacher, with all-natural wood paneling and soft copper light fixtures—an acquaintance of mine led us to a corner table. Joan had a palpable agitation, as if her mind were again frantically working a problem. But as I began to sit, she flashed me an expensive grin. "Aren't you going to wait for me to sit first?"

Which was confusing. I wasn't supposed to feel the slightest bit possessive toward her, or yearning toward her—and I certainly wasn't supposed to "care" in any real sense—and yet I was supposed to be a strong and paternal sort of lover, paying for everything and showing her the utmost respect. "I should hold your chair, too, right?" I asked.

"It wouldn't be a *bad* idea."

"And do you know I'm clueless? I have no idea how to do that stuff."

"Come over here. I'll show you."

"Right here?" I looked around the restaurant, saw the soft-shouldered jackets and good walking shoes and suntanned skin of my hometown's gourmet intelligentsia. Nice people. Smart people. People who didn't worry too much about holding chairs for their dates. "I can't do it, Joan. Just sit down. I'm too self-conscious. But I do want to talk about something. I know you don't want me to, because we're not supposed to be getting to know each other, but I want to talk a little. Because being around you is making me realize that I have a completely confused relationship to formal manners."

"Of course you do."

"You know this."

"You're a mess. But don't tell me about your childhood right now, okay?"

I laughed.

"I was enjoying the fantasy that I could have a boy talk about me absolutely *all* the time."

"Would ninety-nine percent be so bad?"

"No, come on, really. Listen to me first. You never listen to me."

That was absurd.

"And I haven't seen you all day, and I haven't been able to tell anybody my feelings."

"Then tell."

"And this is serious. I really do need to understand why I'm the way I am."

"Honestly, tell me. It's okay."

"But also don't think it means anything, my confiding so much."

"Means anything like what?"

"Like about us."

"Fine."

"I'm not kidding."

"For heaven's sake, Joan. Just talk to me."

It was her father this time—moving onto his yacht after the divorce, putting Joan through visitation weekends of listening to him "fucking his girlfriend in the next cabin." She clearly admired the man—seemed impressed by his emotional self-sufficiency, and even his prowess with women—but she was also furious at him. Joan reserved her most abject hatred and rejection for her mother, whom she saw as an incorrigibly sadistic monster; but she did feel a will to bring her father to heel, to force him to confront how badly he'd blown it as a parent. Like his fucking the babysitter and getting caught, and then moving out and not giving any money or time—except on the rare occasions that he took her along on dates to fancy restaurants. "And I'll admit," Joan said, "that I do still like a nice restaurant. Don't think I'm not grateful for tonight, or that I don't know that it's a stretch for you. I do like it when a man buys me dinner. I'm just saying that it comes out of a pretty sordid period in my life. Half the time, I'd be in the back of his Jaguar trying to read *Harriet the Spy* so I wouldn't see his hand on some tart's thigh, but of course I always did see it, and I'm sure my little brain was going, *Oh, I see, this is how you get Daddy's attention*, and even when he didn't bring a girl, I'd be so self-conscious I'd always call him Daddy in front of the waitresses, so they'd know I wasn't his date. I mean, isn't that sick? That I had to compensate for him in that way?" Joan thought the only way forward, the only way to move beyond all her rage and rejoin her estranged family in California, was to make them face what a disaster her childhood had been. People needed to take responsibility for the damage they'd caused. And then perhaps Joan could finally come home.

Our dinners arrived and while Joan cut into a bloody rack of lamb, once again looking from side to side and occasionally widening her eyes, I wished I could sit beside her and hold her and smooth out the rough edges, encourage forgiving and forgetting.

I picked up my fork and knife and watched the way Joan was eating and tried to copy. I still wanted to tell her about my own childhood, but I could feel that my life was simply not at issue between us. It wasn't part of our contract. She'd put out sex and fun, the deal went, and I'd provide an ear and a warm body in return. "Hey, I know it's a little off-topic," I said, "but can I tell you about this manners business now?"

She tapped a fork on the table like a nervous kid. "I can't necessarily stay at your place tonight, okay?"

"What?"

"I may have to do some stuff with my father in the morning."

"Come on, please just give me your take on this. Okay? Because I'm starting to think it has to do with how divided my family is." I began describing my grandfather, seeking a story line as I went, edging toward the implication that he was much like Joan's father. I said he'd been cut off early from a mother he never liked. He'd worked his way through college and law school by selling men's suits. Then came the war and the bombing runs over occupied France, and then the founding of the big law firm, and the family and the Berlioz in the corner office overlooking the bay, and a Cessna for soaring over the Golden Gate and out to sea, reliving the freedom of the skies. The more I talked, the more impatient Joan grew, her foot bouncing on the floor and her eyes occasionally flitting to the door, so I tried to keep my conversation relevant to her own transition—or at least to my view of it. I told her that my grandfather's life was all about conventional status markers, and while it had brought him great security, there'd been a lot left out. And there was a certain coldness in the guy. I knew what she was maybe going through, I meant to say, and I knew what it was like to admire a man and also to wish he had more room in his heart. This was why my mother had so little self-confidence, I thought—her father just never quite apprehended another human being. He had no capacity for love. So Mom had married a radical-left Irishman and raised her kids in a way that appalled her parents. But she'd been happy. She'd found love and passion. Even though she'd never rejected her father, and she thought I was a lot like him. Apparently he thought so, too. Or that's what Mom said. And I thought maybe I'd always felt caught in between, unsure which way to go. Grandpa or Dad. Grandpa or Dad. Mom loved them both, still called Grandpa "Daddykins" in public, and still made out with my father in plain sight.

"Why are you telling me this?" Joan asked.

I didn't know, exactly, but I was determined to get it all said, to make her listen to me. "It's just that somehow the question of manners versus non-manners—or, rather, holding doors and chairs or not holding doors and chairs—it has some primal ring for me. I'm habituated to the not-holding approach, but I'm surprised by how much I actually enjoy the holding—for you, at least. And it's making me rethink my feelings for my grandfather. I mean, the guy did offer me a chip-off-the-old-block job in his firm, for the summer after my high school graduation, and I quit on day three. That was my ticket to privilege, right? He was really inviting me aboard. He even prepaid a bunch of golf lessons, and I took one and even enjoyed it. Golf's a good time. But see, the problem was that telling my dad, 'Hey, I think I want to become a golfer,' was like saying, 'Gee, Dad, you know what? Fuck you.' So here I am, twenty-nine and changing careers, and wondering what the hell was so wrong about letting the old guy help me out."

"I still don't know why you're telling me this."

"What do you mean?"

She appeared angry now. "What are you trying to accomplish by telling me this?"

"I'm just talking about my life."

"Even though I told you I have no room in my heart."

"I'm not trying to claim any room in your heart. I'm just trying to have a conversation."

"You're trying to get me to agree to something."

"No, I'm not. I'm just saying . . ."

"Opie, you are. Own it. And get the check. I want to go."

I breathed deeply and swallowed my irritation and said, "Okay, maybe I *am* saying something. And maybe it's like this, and don't take it the wrong way, but maybe it's something like 'However I seem right now, like whatever choices I've apparently made, maybe I just want you to know that I'm very much a work in progress, and . . .' "

"Whoa! Opie!"

"What? And why do you keep calling me Opie?"

"Not what we're doing here!"

"What's not?"

"Don't make me do this to you."

"Don't make you what?"

"I'm just some girl you met, right?"

"Meaning?"

"Just say yes."

"Okay, yes. You're just some girl I met."

"And you really can be responsible for your own emotions, right? Like you keep saying? I don't have to feel like you're trying to manipulate me into the very thing I've sworn to avoid?"

"Now I'm the confused one."

"Right, because you're just a sweet kid who never means any harm. So let's forget it. Let's talk about something else."

"What else should we talk about?"

"Well, you could tell me if you think I'm old."

"At twenty-nine?"

"It's an obsession of mine. So just answer. I'm saving you from yourself."

"Old."

"Right. Over the hill. Youth gone by."

"At twenty-nine?"

"Going on thirty. Come on, I know we can do this."

"I guess I'd say you all growed up, baby, but you ain't old."

"Is that your line?"

I lied: "Sure."

"Wow. Maybe you *are* my kind of guy."

I smiled.

"Maybe you do get to take me home for a little while. But you're *really* afraid of my strap-on?"

Joan liked to say that I was a "histrionic bottom" at heart, but that night at my place she demanded that my sex come rough and honest—a curative and half-violent beating she indulged in like free drinks. The longer we made love—"You're finally learning how to fuck me," she said, "it's so great"—and the less I spoke, the more natural she seemed. At ten o'clock, still glancing at her watch, she dug into her postcoital ice cream with the air of a great boxer begrudgingly satisfied—for the moment—with her temporary sparring partner.

"So," she asked later still, bringing a hand towel to her mouth, "a blowjob man."

Having never considered it, and wondering if that sounded too passive—I was an active guy, after all—I mentioned Vicky Freelon and her precocious fellatio.

"And once again, I'm wondering how on earth you decide what to share with me."

"Joan, all I meant was . . ."

"Don't you think I could tell stories?"

"You're right."

"Like about how many boyfriends lived to eat my pussy? How I've had dykes walk up to me in bars, who've heard through the grapevine what a sweet pussy I have, and ask to go down on me?"

"Joan, can I ask you a question? Where did you learn to talk like this?"

"It's the truth."

"Oh, come off it."

"You doubt me?"

"Women in bars."

She nodded.

"And what? You offered yourself up?"

"That's what I'm telling you."

"But how?"

"In the bathroom."

"How, though?"

"Sit on the sink."

"And they'd make you come?"

"Sure."

"No return favor?"

"Or the French waiter I lost my virginity to. You want to hear how he fucked me eighteen times a day?"

"Joan, please. That's physically impossible."

"I was there. So, you want to hear about all that?"

"I just did."

"I just wanted you to know who you were dealing with."

"Got it."

"Good."

"Eighteen?"

She nodded.

"I just can't believe that, because I personally have only . . ."

"I'm telling you, I was there."

"But . . ."

"I need to go home."

"I'll take you."

"But not yet." Joan bore into our sex now like someone try-ing to indulge an unfortunate hunger one final time, as if to be done with it for good. When we were still again, at almost eleven, she said, "Shit, that's maybe even fifty percent."

My shameless heart perked up. "Just fifty?"

She kissed my nose and said, "At least you're improving."

But her testiness never vanished, and around midnight she turned to ask, over a shoulder, "Wait, what did you just say? Did you say just something about my asshole?"

"Ah . . . ass, actually. But I was getting there. Hedging with vagaries."

"Too bad."

"What?"

"It's just too bad."

"Why?"

"Such a white boy."

"What's wrong with being a white boy?"

"Nothing."

"But what's wrong with it?"

"Opie, relax."

"I'm proud of being a white boy. And stop calling me that."

"Relax. Jesus."

"White boys may be evil, but they are not impotent. They did conquer the world."

She stared.

"What?"

"Opie, all I did was upstage you on anal sex."

"It's not like I've never had anal sex."

"Of course it is."

"No, it's not. I can't believe we're having this conversation."

"Let me tell you something. I've been fucked in the ass really well. And if you'd ever done it yourself, you would never have tried it the way you just did. But come on, keep fucking me. You were doing fine."

And then, with her cheek against my own, she said, "Quick: tell me what you're thinking."

I tugged up the comforter and asked what she meant, liking her curiosity.

"While we were having sex. I can feel something, right there. You're hiding from me."

I rubbed my forehead, thinking, *Dig, boy, dig! Unearth the secret self! This is the whole point! She's reaching out to you! She's trying to connect!* "But I'm worried I wasn't thinking about anything at all," I said, pushing onward, trying to avoid the pitfalls of the verbal. But then it came to me, I knew what I was thinking. "I mean, maybe I was just thinking about you, Joan."

"What?"

"Well, I hope this is okay to say, baby, but maybe I was just thinking about how wonderful you feel all around me, surrounding me."

"Oh yuck!" She pulled me back onto her again, as if to make this conversation go away. I tried yet again to find a rhythm that pleased her, and I realized that I'd been right. I'd said exactly what I was thinking.

"Oh Jesus fuck!" she barked now, shoving me off her body and sitting naked against the wall. "It makes me *sick* when you do this."

"When I do what?"

"You were trying not to come, right?"

Oh God.

"It's so creepy and manipulative." She shuddered, and then she began to look for her clothing. "I've got to go, anyway."

Unbelievable.

It was twelve-thirty now, and she didn't have a car. I offered her a ride, but she refused. She said she preferred to call a taxi.

But why?

No reason, she just wanted to take a taxi.

"Joan, let me drive you home."

"Stop pressuring me," she said. "It's really sick."

She was nuts. And ridiculous. And perversely unwilling to see that we were falling for each other. But she also had absolute faith in her perceptions, and she made it abundantly clear if I didn't take them to heart, and look carefully at myself, she'd cut me off for good. And I figured, Fine. I'm not here for love. I'm here for sex, and for whatever Joan seems to know about life and about me. So I apologized, and then I apologized again, and while I walked her down to the street I told her I wasn't doubting her. I just wanted to understand what exactly she was telling me. So that I could be sure not to make the same mistake in the future.

"I can't be here," she said. "I just can't be with you anymore. I keep trusting you to keep your insecurities to yourself, and I'm being a fool."

"But you're not being a fool, Joan. Please don't think that." I seemed to have flipped a switch in Joan, her blood coursing with unhappiness. She stood on the Great Highway, shivering and miserable, looking up and down the empty street. None of this made sense to me, and yet she was so certain. It was as if she saw whole worlds I could not. And even if I was going to keep a lid on my fondness for her, I was still going to have to learn what I always did wrong in these situations, so that I could correct it and not suck and hate myself forever without knowing how to change. Seeing the taxi appear down the block, I apologized yet again and implored her to tell me what on earth was happening. I'd only been trying to please her, I said. I was not a monster. I was not a horrible, cruel person trying to manipulate her. Couldn't she please, please just acknowledge that. Couldn't she concede that I wasn't so evil or shitty or whatever. I just thought we had a sweet thing between us, and I loved being with her, and I had heard everything she'd told me loud and clear. Nothing had changed. I was the same guy who'd listened day and night to her every word. I still knew she had no room in her heart for anybody at all. I still just wanted to pass some time, no strings attached. Please, please, please. I was the same guy she'd been enjoying only minutes ago. But everything out of my mouth was wrong. Everything about me was wrong. When the taxi pulled up beside us, Joan said not to call for a few days.

"A few days?"

"I'm going away. And I need time. I don't want to be bothered. You're going to have to take care of yourself."

"Where are you going?"

"It's none of your business. And if you pester me, and call me whenever you can't control yourself, I will just hate it."

"Joan, please don't do this." There was obviously another guy. Also none of my business.

"Good-bye," she said, closing the taxi door. And just like that, she was gone.

At some level, I had been here before, and I knew that I had to be playing a role in manifesting these crappy exchanges. It takes two to tango, and so forth. But how? What was I doing? Of course there was the recent heartbreak I mentioned, the one that sent me galloping into this no-attachment-dating business to begin with. But there'd also been earlier ones, foundational ones. Like Esther Brukowski, in college. I'd just quit my fraternity—round peg in a square hole, locked in mutual dislike with my brothers—and I'd been anxiously trying to figure out who to be next when I'd met the Jewish golden girl from the Upper West Side. And after three months of bliss and two months of hell—screaming public fights—I'd taken the split so hard that I'd nearly cracked up, and actually sort of stalked her around campus. When I'd finally accepted that she wasn't coming back, I became determined to understand why my truest loves always faltered. I'd gone right to the gender-studies section of the undergraduate library and started reading books with titles like *Women's Ways of Knowing*. From Carol Gilligan's seminal *In a Different Voice*, I'd learned that men and women conceive of morality in different terms. For men, the fundamental wrong is an active infringement on the rights of another: by punching me, you violate my right not to get punched. For women, torts have more to do with the failure to fulfill responsibilities. Which was why men never knew what the hell they'd done so wrong when their girlfriends were mad. But of course this hadn't been much help, and the more relevant example was really the Big Dysfunctional Love Number One, with Vicky Freelon, clear back in the tenth grade. That time, too, I'd been betwixt and between, off my game—having only just transferred to the big public high school. When I met Vicky she became my clique and my world and my sense of self. No matter how bad things got with Vicky, she was all I had, so my attachment only deepened. Even when she declared us "only friends" and then fooled around with a popular water polo player and then "got back together" with me the next day, I'd been right back at her place, watching *Hogan's Heroes* while her wiry-haired father, a straight-toothed, genuinely nice, recently cuckolded deal-maker, fried steaks in the kitchen. And when Vicky sensed that I might be indignant enough to make her pay, and Hogan plotted yet another escape from Stalag 13, and Mr. Freelon chatted with me through the doorless passageway, she undid my specially tapered peg-legged Levi's.

"So, what grade are you in, Mr. Harper?"

"Ah . . ."

Vicky's deft, expert fingers fiddled through the zipper.

"What's that, son?"

"Tenth. I'm in tenth grade."

Blue TV screen light bathed my little pinkness, while Vicky leaned over and held back her crucifix and treated my little pecker like the very joystick of my self-control, as if whatever resistance I had bottled up inside, whatever judgment of her or glimmering of pride, could be worked and worked like the cursor in a video game, until all the fire poured out and the guns went empty.

"And did Vicky say you guys have a class together?"

Oh dear God.

And if Vicky's father had walked into that room and seen what no father should ever see—well, goddamn it. Because by the time I'd watched little Vicky pause to call out, "Hey, can Harper stay for dinner?" I was a goner. I had discovered that, yes, erotic gratification was indeed an immutable force in my inner life. And so I stopped even trying to fight, and struggled instead to prove my trustworthiness, but because I was incapable of understanding all the ways in which I was a loser, I had no means of triumphing in the contest that I'd set for myself, the one in which I could finally stop sucking and start feeling good inside. So I started playing an awful lot of electric guitar with the lights out, writing heavy metal songs with titles like "Genocide," and contemplating killing myself, enslaved as I was by my own lameness and by the fickle and vindictive drug of her love and her lips. And then came the afternoon that I lay fully clothed atop Vicky's bed, on my back, with Vicky astride me. She wore a long skirt that day, and she had a new Devo album on the tape deck. A knock at the bedroom door: Mr. Freelon, home early.

Vicky said calmly, "Wait a sec, Daddy."

I began to sit up, expecting her to hop off me.

"Stay still," she whispered, somehow choosing that of all moments to give me what I wanted most of all. Pulling her plaid skirt so that it draped entirely over my clothed stomach and lap, she reached under to unzip my Levi's, pulled aside her pink Hello Kitty panties, and slipped me at long last into the moist heat of her life-affirming creation, the greatest sensation of my short life and quite clearly the whole reason for my existence. Putting her skirt back in place to hide all evidence of our coupling, she called out, in her very best good-girl voice, "Okay, Daddy, you can come in now."

The door opened and there stood miserable Mr. Freelon, having already changed out of his three-piece Realtor's suit and into his candy-striped nylon running shorts, Nike trainers, and tank top. A real adult who'd been jogging a lot, replacing alcohol with endorphins, he was stopped for a moment by wondering what was going on beneath that skirt, and doubtless also by the chaos of expressions flitting across my young face. But then Mr. Freelon chose to ignore his instincts and pretend that he suspected nothing. Breaking into a weird smile, he strode into the room. I can't even guess what my eyes were doing, but I do know that I had zero space in the brain for anything but the ecstatic miracle that was happening and the bewildering circumstances in which it was taking place, Vicky's boiling hot ocean enveloping the happy little fish that was me, while her half-oblivious father pulled up the little-girl desk chair, crossed his hairy legs, folded his ropy arms, and looked directly into my eyes. Who knew why, but Mr. Freelon then calmly asked about my newest skateboard and chuckled with a perverse, unconscious giddiness, while Vicky rocked faintly to bring me closer to that easy little boy's ejaculation, and the very face of her father's impotence loosened every muscle in my body.

Could it cause lasting damage to a boy's mind, I'd wondered since, *to taste the real forbidden fruit so early and with such perfect dramaturgy as to include the on-looking eye of the very personification of the forbidding god himself? To have the Hellenic reunion of sex so thoroughly affirm my primacy over a depressed, doubly cuckolded guy who only wanted to be a part of his crazy kid's life and was instead sitting there in a miniature, butterfly-painted chair pretending this snot-nosed, low-rent punk was rolling his eyes back only because he was so thrilled by the new German bearings in his red Kryptonics downhill wheels?*

But the more salient question was whether this really *was* a cautionary tale, a prophetic parable I'd do well to heed. Vicky, after all, had lived for the heart medicine of sex every bit as much as Joan and I, and our copulation had likewise become a daily need, the balm of her body if not the affirmation of her trust (that being the only thing that could have made me feel like a single, intact personality) available during every alleyway lunch period and every long afternoon. Night after sleepless night, I'd snuck out of my parents' house and skateboarded lickety-split across town, indulging in Bataan death marches of straight-eighth and pounding quarter notes until we were both raw and sore and lost in passion, wearing hickey necklaces to school and drawing pornography on desks and lying about it, all inhibition falling away at precisely the age when it should have held us in its reassuring grip. Craven for closeness with my girl, hating my own cravenness, hating her for being its object, I'd blown off all my friends and put heart and soul into humping away by the hour and the day, as if eros were a riveting coma from which I could not wake up. And just as with Joan, all these fifteen years later—my emotional architecture seemingly frozen in amber—there'd been these same ridiculous performance concerns: could I fuck as long as the last boyfriend? As hard? As many times in a twenty-four-hour period? And what about the ending? Was this what I should expect? After nearly a year of escalating insanity, during which I'd lost all notion of who I was and descended into complete addiction to Vicky's pussy and caprices and to my own lunacy, Vicky's doorbell finally tolled for me. I answered to find a tan boy in stone-washed jeans and a distressed-leather bomber jacket asking for my gal.

"She's here," I said. "But who are you?"

"I'm Eric. Are you her brother?"

He had to be from a rival high school. "I'm her boyfriend," I said.

"Oh well, could I talk to her?"

"Wait in the kitchen," Vicky told me. "I'll be right back."

Ten minutes passed, then fifteen. I stepped onto the porch, where they sat together, fog blowing in.

"I told you to wait inside," Vicky snapped.

Right. I did as told. Which would have been fine, except that sex stitches people together willy-nilly. Every screw sets a single, slender strand between hearts, and adolescent hearts above all—I had by then become love and become my need for Vicky, having thought of nothing else for ages, having learned to fill the hole in me only by filling the one in her, having dreamed that she was a tragically fallen but truly marvelous girl in need of saving, and that I was the boy-hero for the job, and that my success was a matter of my own spiritual life or death. I was too far gone, in other words, too deep in the abyss of our ritual adoration and abuse ever to hope for a healthy extrication.

Back inside Vicky's gracious living room, with its stuffy antiques and that black leather couch and the massive cabinet television, another ten minutes passed, then ten more. Stepping into the green-themed kitchen, I fingered a wine bottle, then a chair, then a chopping knife. Then Vicky returned and asked what my problem was, and I couldn't even tell her off. So I just set the knife down and told her I thought we should probably break up, and then I walked out. That was the best I could do. And she actually clapped and laughed and cheered—a humiliation akin to having my skin ripped off, showing bleeding weak muscles to all the laughing world. I hated being such a weakling, pussy-whipped freak, his girl actually happy for him when he finally crawls away, nursing his wounds. I surfed alone for nearly a year straight, finding myself at last while the tan boy haunted me and Vicky's powder-blue BMW appeared everywhere, her Body Shop China Rain perfume on every girl on every corner, nobody allowed to mention her in my presence. Then I bumped into her at the Savoy-Tivoli, a Euro-teen café and bar in the old Italian district of North Beach. She was very drunk and wound up on cocaine, and she said she missed me and thought I was the sweetest person. And here was the really bad part, the incriminating part, equally as disturbing as the groveling and yearning: I'd found myself asking if Vicky would blow me in the bathroom, and when she said she would—"Anything, baby, anything, please," and that she'd even swallow—I'm afraid that I said, "I bet you would. Fuck off, huh?" Not attractive, not healthy, not a contributing factor to a happy existence. This had also been my only prior experience with talking dirty, and was perhaps responsible for my shyness on the subject with Joan. My cowardly anger, when I found the courage to let it out, was so mysteriously excessive and ugly. And yet even now, while writhing apart from Joan and wondering when she'd return and if she'd call, I still carried this idiotic certainty that *these* were somehow the real loves, and that beyond these sorry dramas lay the fusion of hearts and bodies that a man could at last believe to be the genuine article. And it was that certainty, and that capacity for lunatic attachment, I now felt, that I had to kill forever.

Joan's return was more bewildering than her explosion: no apology, no "Gee, I guess I overreacted," and no interest in agreeing on a mutually respectful understanding of what had happened. All that was required, she implied, for us to move forward, was for me to drive over and visit her and to acknowledge in person that I had been a complete ass and that our fight had been entirely my fault, and to promise that it would never happen again. When I dared to ask where exactly she'd been, she said to call back when I was ready to be a grown-up. She was claiming absolute freedom of action and would brook no restraint. And I reminded myself yet again that this was her prerogative, she'd never told me otherwise, and she was in a lot of pain. I had to erase all thoughts of a future with her—all my fantasies of marrying her, and feeling so outrageously proud of my beauty, and fucking her up and down every wall of our house for the rest of our lives—but that didn't mean I couldn't head across town with a bouquet of daisies, find her at the Cavanaugh place, and hang on a little longer in order to learn just a little bit more. Which was a good thing, because once I arrived, I was instantly happy to be there. I was nuts about Joan. I didn't just love everything about the way she looked, I loved the very sound of her voice and the way she smelled and the quick dart of her dark brown eyes. I liked her wit and humor and effusiveness and lunatic will to have fun. And she seemed genuinely happy to see me, too, and tender and vulnerable and eager to reunite. We hugged and kissed and took a long walk in silence, and we necked on the sidewalk. In our days apart, she said with excitement, she'd realized that it really was time to move back home, to stop running away from her family and her childhood. She wanted to be clear that I was not at all a factor in the decision—"It's very important that you know that and accept it, so you don't derail me with some big relationship I shouldn't be in"—but also that she'd booked a flight to New York for the evening after next, to collect her belongings and close down her affairs, and she was half-wondering if I shouldn't come along. For fun. For the hell of it. And that was fine with me. That was what I was all about. Doing things for fun. No attachment, no commitment. But first, Joan needed to hear that apology, and because we apparently weren't trying to have a "big relationship"—or any proper relationship at all— I decided that asking her to share blame would be a blunder. She would only explode and disappear again. So I swallowed deeply, and told myself things would not always be like this between us, and admitted it all. "You're right," I said, "I'm surprisingly immature for my age. I'm only just starting to realize it, but I think it's good for me to see it. And I really do hear everything you tell me about expecting nothing, and how you can't be responsible for another heart. I also do see—honestly, truly—that my attempts to withhold orgasm and facilitate yours are repulsively controlling and emblematic of everything that's wrong with me and that always has been wrong with me. I see perfectly—I promise I do, and I'm not just saying this to curry favor, which I agree is a bad tendency of mine—that my behavior in bed infuriates you because it really is sort of calculating, even though I've never realized it, and it really is a means of trying to coerce dependency and approval from women, and that's doubtless why a lot of women have fled me in the past, and I see also that my blithe ignorance of this, my assumption that my actions are essentially good and well meant is an almost sociopathic amorality born of my mother's absurdly overweening and indiscriminate love."

Joan wasn't just content to listen, either; she needed to egg me on, to push harder and harder at all the reasons why she could not even consider mutual commitment. As if clawing at some scab in herself, she was soon encouraging me to see that my relationship with my mother wasn't nearly as close or warm as I imagined, that my father's politics and thus my own were based on a fear of failure and an unwillingness to compete rather than on any genuinely held values, and that my ongoing affection for Bernie and Eliza was rooted in nothing but a belief that they were socially advantageous people to know. Which was not inconceivable, when I really considered it. They had a wide circle of friends, after all, and created a wonderfully complete social world around themselves. I would befriend anyone, Joan felt, from whom I thought I could benefit, and should, in fact, be more honest with myself and figure out how to achieve the wealth and social status that *I*—not she!—found so compelling. And when I felt thoroughly beaten down and sad and lousy, she got to what was really on her mind: whatever dark secret I'd learned from Bernie and Eliza.

"Very little," I said, wishing Joan had more common sense than this.

"Don't bullshit me."

"But why go there? Why insist on hearing such things?"

"If I'm going to live here, and especially if I'm going to spend time with you, I need to know what I'm dealing with."

"Joan, it'll ruin my friendship with Eliza forever. They talked to me in confidence that day."

"Then it must be really bad. So now you can either tell me or forget about ever seeing me again."

I wanted to hug Joan. I wanted to hold her close. I wanted to tell her that she was a lovely person and needn't worry so much about the opinions of others.

"Come on, Eliza poisoned you against me somehow, and I know it."

"Joan, she just said you were a little complicated. That's all."

"Complicated."

I nodded.

"That's a polite way of calling someone an asshole, isn't it? Out with the rest."

There was no stopping Joan, and I didn't have the will to put my foot down. I cared more about avoiding another rupture. So I came out with a little more: something about Joan's boss and her boss's boss in New York, maybe a pattern of older European men.

"What else?"

Sex on an oyster shell, the need for a nice American boy.

"A nice American boy."

"That's right. Pretty ridiculous, I know."

"I hate nice American boys."

I chuckled, stung.

"And don't think I haven't had a lot of them. And I am not sex on an oyster shell, either. I don't even think about sex. I never think about sex."

"I know you don't."

"What else?"

"That's it."

"There's something else. You're not done."

"Joan, let's stop here, okay? This is really poison."

"You're not done."

Okay, the hell with it. I told her: Bernie says you tried to seduce him in front of Eliza, which is ridiculous, I know, and he probably didn't mean it.

"And you believed this?"

"I just didn't think about it one way or another. I was acutely conscious of hearing things I shouldn't be hearing."

"But you believed it. You believed I actually tried to seduce my oldest friend's boyfriend, right in front of her face."

"I didn't know you. I'd never even seen you."

"Why didn't you tell me this sooner?"

"Are you crazy?"

"You've been carrying it around, waiting to see if I'm some kind of psycho. I could kill Eliza."

"She didn't tell me that last thing."

"It doesn't matter. It's her story. I'm going to have to slam her."

"Wait, please. Please don't do that. You'll really betray my confidence if you do that."

"Eliza doesn't learn if you don't slam her. She's always seen me as this big sexualized creature, from the time we were like thirteen, which is insane. It's just her own jealousy about me, and her desire for me. She's always had this secret crush on me, like she couldn't decide if she wanted to fuck me or be me. And I wasn't thinking about any of that. I was always just envying her and looking up to her and believing everything she said about who I was and what I should do with my life, because she had everything I didn't have. She actually had a normal family where everybody loved each other, so she thought she could just tell me who I was. And then she'd act like I was the one who had everything. You're the same way, too. You're so spoiled with hippie love from your hippie mother that you can't even wipe your own nose."

When Joan had expended the last of her anguish—this story had touched a nerve—she announced the need to buy a hat. We walked in a steady drizzle down to Haight Street, past a townhouse I'd lived in with my folks when I was a baby, before the move to Berkeley. We were just back from the South then, and our VW van got stolen by a gang of bad flower children. (The switch from acid to speed as drug-of-choice had darkened things in a big hurry.) I guess Dad saw two of the hippie hoods on the street the very next day playing with his camera, so what did he do? A thirty-five-year-old husband and father? He grabbed these guys by the collar and dragged them back to the apartment and made them sit on the couch while Mom served them orange juice, and he told them they had an hour to make his VW show up in the street outside or he was calling the cops. There I was asleep in my crib, or playing with a truck, or drooling, or whatever I was doing, and an hour later the van was on the street, albeit with the upholstery slashed and "Fuck you" spray-painted on the outside.

In a narrow little clothing store, I watched Joan try on blouses, all to great effect.

"Eliza's half-right," Joan called from behind a dressing-room curtain. "You know that, don't you?"

"About what?" I was sitting on the back seat of an American sedan, now bolted to an unfinished wooden floor.

"I do have some really stupid patterns with older men. How's this blouse look?"

"Stunning." It was a gauzy, short-sleeved, violet-colored thing, largely transparent.

"You sure? You say that about everything."

"Everything does look stunning on you, but that especially."

"You like it, then."

"I do."

"I guess I'm buying it, cause that's all I've got to go on

right now." She bought a close-fitting, loosely knit crocheted cap, too.

"You know that's a Joni Mitchell hat?" I said. "From *Miles of Aisles*?"

Turning away from the bustling, ridiculous Haight-Ashbury and all its ice cream stores and head shops, we walked into quiet uphill neighborhoods and Joan told me what she'd meant: the way she'd met her first boyfriend, for example. "I was eating dinner with my family at a Basque place on Broadway," she said, taking long, weary strides up a steep hill.

"Le Bateau Rouge?" My parents loved that place.

"No. Another one. Anyway."

"I'm sorry. I really do want to hear this."

She cleared her throat. "There was this other family there that we knew, but we hadn't seen them in a long time, and I wrote my phone number on a piece of paper to pass it to them, and this waiter, this French guy named Paul, thought it was for him. He thought I was secretly slipping him my phone number."

Eliza was so right about Joan: X-ray vision about everyone else, oblivious to herself. This story was ridiculous. "But weren't you actually slipping him your number?"

"Of course not. I was eighteen."

"Your first boyfriend? At eighteen?"

"Oh yeah. See, this is this whole fantasy you have about me, which is very flattering, but it's ridiculous. I was just a soccer player in high school. I was not *raw sex*. Anyway, when I reached out to pass my number . . ."

"You had your own number?"

"Yeah. Anyway, he just swooped in and took it. And it would have been fine. He was absolutely staggeringly gorgeous." She bit her lip at the memory.

"Really?"

"Ooh." She shook her head. "He was *unfuckingbelievable* to look at. He was dumb as a doornail, too, which was a pity, but he had a great accent, and he was the perfect guy to lose my virginity to. Eliza was speechless with jealousy. Except that then I never went off to college, so instead of just having this little summer fling with an older European guy, which is exactly what every little girl in Pacific Heights wants . . ."

"How old was he?"

"He was twenty-six. But I didn't go anywhere, right? I just went up to Davis, where my parents went. It was horrible, and he got so possessive, and it was like I never went to college."

"You mean in terms of football games and sororities and all that?"

"Yeah, or instead of going to Brown, and dating J.F.K., Jr., and interning at *The New Yorker*, I was like not eating, and sneaking into the kitchen at night to play with knives, and nobody noticed."

"Cutting yourself?"

"And getting way too skinny. My whole family was right there and nobody noticed. I'd go home and try to tell my mother, and I just couldn't. She was too caught up in her own misery, and I couldn't put that on her, too. There was no way she could handle it. And my dad was just a joke. You want to know what a joke my father was? You know what we usually did on my rare afternoons with him? We went to the golf course so I could hang out in the clubhouse while he hit eighteen holes."

"The Great Pacific Golf Club?" I asked.

She nodded.

"I told you I lived in the ghetto, you just weren't listening. It's not about how much money you have, or what school you go to. It's about love and not getting it. And I was not getting it, and I knew it. And Eliza has to turn that into a bad thing.

You know that ménage à trois idea? That's *her* fantasy, not mine. And she's had it since high school. I didn't even date boys in high school. I only had one lover before Paul and she was the other prettiest girl in our school and Eliza wanted to see it as some big, wild sexual thing. Which it wasn't. This girl was just exquisitely beautiful and we were both on the soccer team and she really loved me. We saw each other for years, too. But I was just a soccer player, and a great student. I knew my only hope of getting out of this sick family was to propel myself to the other side of the country for college, and I did it. I got perfect grades, I was on four varsity sports from my freshman year—my freshman year, the basketball coach let me start in varsity games without even showing up for practice because I was running on the cross-country team. And all this shit started happening with men because I got sideswiped. I was getting recruited from every Ivy League school to play soccer, and something happened."

She stopped walking now to look at a pretty little garden behind a black wrought-iron fence. The drizzle had stopped and blue shone through the clouds here and there. I asked what it was that had happened—this was actually one of the central miseries of Joan's life, and yet an unexplained one, some painful, particular moment when her whole glorious plan for her life had evaporated.

"I don't really know," she said, her voice trailing into uncertainty.

"But what are you referring to?"

"I got all these letters from like Yale and Brown saying, 'We had every intention of admitting you this year, but certain things have come to light which render this impossible.' "

What on earth?

"One of the counselors at my high school apparently wrote a letter at the last minute telling all these places not to take me."

"And killed every one of your applications?"

She nodded.

"What on earth?"

"I really have no idea."

But how could that be true? How could she have no idea?

Joan looked at the back of her left hand. "But that's when it really happened. That's when I crawled into a cave that I didn't come out of. That I still haven't come out of. And I was just a soccer player before all that, you know? I really was. I didn't even think about men. I mean, I always knew I was pretty—like, when I was a little girl I broke my collarbone and the doctors went out of their way to set it properly, knowing that you don't squander beauty like that."

I nodded, increasingly disoriented.

"But it wasn't until I went to Europe that all this stupid shit with men started." She'd gone first when she was little, because of her parents' divorce, which had been triggered, as it turned out, by Joan herself coming down from the TV room to get a snack and finding her mother on the kitchen floor with the carpenter. "They were locked together like crabs," Joan told me, demonstrating with her hands and with a disgusted expression on her face. "I was just like, 'Oh, huh.' Then I turned around and went back up to the TV room and sat down next to my brother, and after a while my mom came and sat next to me and watched TV for a while. It was pathetic. And then she went back downstairs and I kept watching TV. My dad, too. My brother just told me this year that he walked in on Dad with the babysitter. I was like, 'No way, I saw Mom with the carpenter.' " In the aftermath, Mrs. Artois had taken the kids to Greece for a month and then rented an apartment in Paris and a villa on the Riviera for the summer. Europe had come to be, as far as I can tell, the place where life was glamorous and new for Joan instead of miserably complicated. She felt absolutely at home there in a way she'd never felt at home in America, so in college she went back every chance she got—for every summer and all of her junior year—and somewhere in there Joan's sense of herself had begun to change, from wholesome, sexless athlete to object of desire. "Everyone in Europe," she said, "wanted to marry me all of a sudden. Like princes, you know?"

I laughed at this, and she laughed with me. "I know it's ridiculous," she said. "It really must sound ludicrous. But it's actually true. You wouldn't believe it, how many marriage proposals I've gotten. Naval officers, captains of industry, heads of state, old men, young men. And I probably should've accepted a couple. I just got so sick of being the wanted one. I wanted to do the wanting myself. And why *shouldn't* I marry a prince, anyway?"

"Are you really asking me that?" It was all such a loony cartoon, and yet Joan spoke as if perfectly serious. It made me both more nervous about her and more fond of her; I was starting to see the protective bubble she'd built for herself. I was starting to see how dearly she needed a safe and secure love.

"I don't know," she said. "I guess I really am asking you that." She sat down suddenly on the sidewalk under a plum tree.

I was not a millionaire myself, of course, and I'd been ordered to expect nothing and feel nothing, so the question was confusing. But it offered the chance to be a dispassionate friend. To help Joan think about her life without injecting my own agenda. And at least I was earning her confidence, and that could only stitch us closer together. I was also oddly charmed— her narrative's absurdity struck me as sweet and vulnerable.

"Really," she said. "Why shouldn't I marry a prince?" Her voice had become vaguely childlike now.

"An actual prince?"

"Princes are good things."

We both laughed.

"You really could, couldn't you?"

She nodded. "Yep, it's the brutal truth."

On this point, I half-believed her. "You could just show up in the right resorts with the right clothes and pull in a millionaire?"

"I really could."

"You'd even know what resort to go to and what to wear."

She thought for a moment, lips pressed together, then nodded with a laugh. "Oh my God," she said. "I've had such a weird life. But yeah. I know exactly where I'd go. I could get a plane tonight." She shook her head and smiled. "You don't know how important money is," Joan told me, looking up now like a child from the ground. "Come down here and sit with me." She pulled me to her side and said with great weariness, "You really don't. Believe me: it makes a big goddamn difference. I mean, what am I supposed to do," she said in her sweetest five-year-old's voice, holding one of my hands with both of hers, "when I really like a boy and he's not rich?"

I just looked at her, utterly confused. What the hell was she saying?

"I'm being serious now," she said, though she wasn't really. "Aren't you maybe going to do something really clever and make a million dollars?"

Somehow, this too charmed me to pieces. "I have no idea, sweetheart. I might, I really might. But it'd be a big mistake to count on it." I tried to think of a way, and couldn't, but who knew? Who could say what a person might do or become? So I experimented and told Joan that I didn't think she was looking for a sugar daddy, that she wouldn't have gone to Peru and stayed in California all this time. Though I really had no idea what Joan was doing or looking for, I told her what I hoped—that she was looking for something altogether different now, and that she didn't want to be some banker's kept jewel, sleep-walking through an endless, dreary round of formal baloney with people she didn't know. I told her she was more than that.

"But I like that baloney," she said with a smile. "Don't think I don't. I was the queen of the debutantes in high school."

"You were a real debutante?"

"I didn't actually go to the cotillion—my mom wouldn't let me. She thought it was cheap. But yeah. And see, even *that's* not my life anymore. Nothing's ever my life for long enough. It's that thing about half-lives. I was in the Junior Olympics for soccer, and then I just stopped playing in college. Why did I do that? Because I was depressed, I guess. And then graduate school, which I guess I'm glad I quit, but all this stuff I'm dealing with now, my job in New York and this guy I was in love with there. Fucking Eliza, I'm telling you."

"Your boss?"

"I was in love with this man. And I guess I shouldn't have been." Gujie was apparently the president of the European division of the company. They'd met at a shoot in Venice—Joan's first overseas casting job—and Joan said she hadn't been at all attracted, but let him take her out to dinner when he was in New York, or when she was in London for the company. "I was sick of being poor," she said, "and I was sick of artsy struggle—you think I'm so materialistic, but I'd been with a history professor for three years before Gujie—and I just thought, Wow, I could be done, with this guy." She admitted that she'd been a sucker for the lavish weekends in Vienna and Rome, for the flower deliveries and surprise visits and his family homes on the Normandy coast and in Paris's sixteenth arrondissement, near L'Arc de Triomphe. There'd even been those architect's drawings of the home he would build for just the two of them, on

Majorca, and talk of a big San Francisco wedding. As in any provincial American city, San Francisco society places a high premium on titled European mates, and Gujie even delivered there, after a fashion—he'd recently been honored by the French government for his contributions to the film industry. Things had begun to get complicated when Joan's immediate boss in New York, a former director from England, began to pursue her. Fifty years old, married, and the father of a boy exactly Joan's age, he'd only been looking for company. His family was all in London, after all, and he was so lonely, and he and Joan had so much in common. ("I loved him," Joan admitted, "but I wasn't *in* love with him. He was a beautiful man.") While working on a period piece set in South America, this man had insisted on buying Joan dinner after work, taking her to his apartment for the viewing of endless relevant films by great directors—she was getting an extraordinary education, having the most dazzling conversations with this man. But then he'd begun calling on weekends, trying to find out if she was available; he even confessed that he was no longer in love with his wife and could think of nothing but Joan. She'd told him many, many times about Gujie, but he didn't seem to care, and he was her boss, after all. Soon Gujie was involved: furious and jealous, demanding that Joan report this man to personnel. Eventually, prodded by Gujie and a roommate she now considered a traitor, Joan went to the company's chief personnel officer.

"She was terrified of me," Joan remembered now, still sitting on the sidewalk. "I guess she thought I was going to bring a lawsuit or something." Joan had been reassigned immediately, at a higher rank, with higher pay, and yet in a division that meant nothing to her: Asia-Pacific marketing. The sacrifice of her dream job felt worthwhile, of course, because soon enough she and Gujie would marry and she'd quit and move to Europe with him. Then the ax fell: Gujie called on the eve of a flight to visit her in New York. He'd fallen in love, he said, with a student who had been renting a room in his house. He was very sorry. Joan was destroyed, and immediately reevaluated her life: she had always wanted to act but had never had the confidence for it. In high school, in her senior year, she'd auditioned for the lead in the school presentation of *Cabaret*, and had landed the part with no training at all. She'd made her mother promise not to come, but on opening night, when she stepped out onto the stage, she saw her mother standing in the back of the hall and fell mute. Now she wanted to try again, and she decided she would go straight to the top: she would apply to Yale's graduate program, the most exclusive in the country. Hating her now very corporate job by day, she worked on monologues and applications by night, and then Gujie appeared at her door: he had made the biggest mistake of his life, he declared, and wanted to try again.

"What can I say?" Joan asked. "I loved him. I really did." Several delirious New York weekends later, she'd finally assented to a Paris visit. She would leave immediately after her audition at Yale—just take a cab straight to the airport. For that last week, she took every acting workshop she could get into, and then took the train up to New Haven and sat in that long, long line. Watched one disappointed face after another emerge from the theater. Moments before her turn, she called Gujie for moral support, and a woman answered the phone. Yep: he'd done it again. The theater doors opened, Joan's name was called, and she walked in there and blew their minds, had every present faculty member in open, weeping tears by the end of her delivery. "We can't admit you," they told her, "because you just don't have enough experience, but we want you to know that you are genuinely very talented, and you absolutely should not give up on an acting career." They were stunned, Joan told me. She had walked out of the audition, picked up her luggage, and gone to the airport, anyway, just as she'd planned. She'd stood around in the departures lounge for a while, looking at destinations, and finally settled on home.

"And that's when I met you?"

"About three days later."

"Ouch."

"You getting the picture now?"

"I'm getting the picture." And what I saw was that Joan was even more lost than I'd known, and that she really had had a pretty screwy life, and that she was genuinely doing her best to confront it. I also saw that all her talk of personal transformation was a form of wishful thinking, and that despite it all, I was falling in love with her. I was falling in love with the whole idea of being her strong caretaker, master of this half-broken jewel.

"And please," she said, "please, *please* don't think you're going to save me, okay? I can't bear it."

I laughed, felt known.

"I've got to save myself this time." A dog had found us now, and Joan settled into a paroxysm of petting and mumbling the dog equivalent of baby talk, rubbing her face into this brown Labrador's face, scratching its belly. Then she saw its owner—a woman about Joan's age—and slapped the dog on the ass to send him off. "I just feel like maybe I'm permanently broken," Joan said, watching wistfully as the woman put the dog back on a leash. "And that's just it. It's all over. My whole life's going to be one big near-miss like that, you know?"

"You are *not* broken," I told her, though of course I suspected she was, if such a thing were possible. I felt that in her prior incarnation she never would have given me the time of day.

"Are you sure? I think maybe I *am* broken."

"All this just makes you a stronger person."

"That's what Eliza's mom used to say. She'd say, 'Joanie, you'll be made of steel.' But I don't *want* to be made of steel. I want to made of soft things, you know? Nice things."

The next morning, with her New York flight scheduled for the subsequent day, Joan encouraged me to cancel my teaching and drive her up the coast for another farewell night away. A few days of sunshine had brought out the green grass and the early flowers, and we took a hike above a Zen monastery, picture-perfect organic crop rows and elegant little wooden Zendo (no nails, only wooden pegs), and a big soothing halo of spiritual peace. Joan breathed in the blue sky and loved the views, the soft winter warmth, and I suppressed my curiosity about how long she'd be gone and whether she'd been serious about having me visit. I knew now that I was involved with a nut, but I felt that I was involved with a glorious and mysterious nut, and one who could make a man profoundly happy if she tried. At a private patch of meadow, a profusion of red paintbrush and yellow oxalis, orange poppies and purple lupine, we ate lunch and chatted, and Joan surprised me by raising again the possibility of my coming to New York. I would never have mentioned it myself, for fear of seeming to pressure her, and I did not jump at the idea now. But she was insistent, she wanted a firm yes, and I gave it. She wouldn't be firm about when, because she wasn't sure exactly how long she'd be there. "Definitely not right away, because I'm going to be dealing with so, so much. And I really don't know where my head will be. But we'll be in touch, okay?"

With the sun well past zenith, Joan said, "Now, here's the thing: you fuck me like that, and I love it so, so much—seventy-five percent, easy—and then I'm drifting off in the sun, and I'm worrying that maybe my mother didn't actually love my brother and me. I mean, imagine thinking that, during sex. And of course, you're right. I'm learning to believe the things you say, because you do seem to have a good heart. Like I'm open to the idea that my mother loved me at some level. Or that she does now, anyway. Mothers have to love their children, right? Although I'd still like to learn about this demonstrative love you apparently got, and which, yes, darling, yes, you do know how to bathe me in. But come on, I'm talking. Get your face out of there. You know you're not allowed. And I need to be reminded yet again that you're not just here because I'm a great lay or because you think I'm such a rich girl." And so on: nobody in her dance classes having a clue how often she told the secretary, "No, ma'am, I don't need a taxi this evening, I do promise my daddy will pick me up soon." Nobody understanding how it felt to find her mother lying on the couch with an empty wine bottle. "She'd stare at me with her big, feline eyes," Joan said, mad at the memory, "and not speaking a word. It scared the daylights out of me, as if my mother were slipping off the planet. And all I really wanted her to say was 'I love you,' you know? Just once? So I'd cry to her about something that happened with my friends, or I'd ask her to sign school papers, and she'd stare at me like I was a rosebush. It was so useless, and I think maybe that's how I got to be such a drama queen. I started making up outlandish stories to get her attention, like, 'Okay, an F in English doesn't get a rise out of you? How about if I say my brother burned me with a cigarette on purpose? No? Well, you know, my voice coach fingered me after class today.' That's why I'm such a good liar. My mother was letting herself die before my eyes, and I wanted to rescue her, but you can't when you're a kid. And you shouldn't have to. It's not your responsibility, and my mother needs to face this. I couldn't even cry and scream because I still had to make myself dinner and make my lunch for the next day, and I'd always get in some fight with my brother where he'd bend me over and shove my face in the toilet. And even then, my mother was pathetic. If she tried to stop him, he'd beat her up, too."

"Did he really shove your face in the toilet?" What the hell was she telling me?

"Do you think I'm making this up?"

"Of course not, but the image you just . . ."

"Why do you ask questions like that?"

"Sorry, sorry . . ."

She reached down to put her hands in my hair and said, "Okay, I got to tell you something, baby. I still can't figure out what you're looking for down there."

"What do you mean?"

"There's no clitoris on your tongue, right?"

"There doesn't have to be. It just pleasures me to pleasure you."

"Ooo, I don't believe in that kind of thing. Isn't it just an excuse to get a girl all lubed up?"

"Think Leda and the Swan, on the mountaintop."

"What's with all the mythology? And Zeus rapes Leda, anyway."

"Please?"

"You really, really want to?" She looked around at the orange poppies and then touched my pleading face. "It's so much to ask." She was smiling, so I laughed and she said, "But you know what I'd *really* love, then?"

"Tell me."

"Oh, this is going to sound so weird."

"Try me."

"Please don't laugh, okay? I'm so fragile today."

"I would never laugh."

"What I've really been wanting? Is if I could be *little* Joanie."

"Anything at all."

"Kind of a pure thing I keep wanting to share with you." She rolled on the blanket and said, "Kind of . . . like when you're five years old and playing in the summertime, and you don't know your body's there or what it means, because it's all you are, and you, you're like an older guy I don't even know, but I really trust you . . ." The afternoon sea blew a gentle breeze through the grass. "Like an older guy. And I don't know maybe what's going on, but it's pure, not gross." Her voice flickered with anxiety. "What?"

"Nothing." This made me very happy, and more than a little nervous.

She said, "You're thinking something."

"I'm not thinking anything. Really, I'm not."

"Cash, please understand what I'm saying, about it's pure."

I nodded, all calm reassurance, and she lay back like a perfect actress vanishing into her role, bringing up from the waters of herself this delicate girl-goddess. It was a feat I envied and admired, and also found unsettling. Gazing lazily into the green grass, she seemed lost in the sanctity of her own self-exposure. *Love*, I thought. *I think I might actually be falling in love. At last, this most exquisitely sexual and vulnerable girl-woman shows herself to me.* A naked-faced buzzard flew low overhead and Joan's eyes followed as if it were a dove in a harmless sky. My lungs filled with the fecundity of spring, and I heard Joan humming, relaxed and without self-consciousness. I kissed her toes and feet, hyperalert to my every thought, careful not to leak the slightest false note—lest I should scare her away. I kissed her ankles and her calves, the backs of her knees, and Joan pulled lazily at a willow leaf. The sun burned my neck and an insect clattered in the grass.

"Get off me," Joan said.

"What?"

"I don't want to do this anymore." Her eyes darted around. I was on my knees.

"Move," she said. "Come on." She reached for her shorts.

Oh, for God's sake.

"Are you going to let me get my shorts or not?" Her voice was threatening now, shaking.

I sat away from her.

"You think this is some kind of pedophilia fantasy. Right?"

Wasn't it one?

Fumbling with her shorts, Joan started for the trail, marching fast to the Econoline. "You are such a rapist," she said over a shoulder. "And you don't even know it. Tricking me into revealing myself, just so you can feel good about yourself and then tell everybody about tweaky girl number 415 and how kinky the sex was." While I struggled to stay abreast, half-jogging on the dirt road, a hawk kited on the evening breeze. I desperately wanted not to lose her quite yet, and I told Joan she was right, she was absolutely right, because I felt sure that was the case. I said I was so sorry. Please forgive. Please don't shut me out. Please. "I'm the one you can trust, remember? I'm the one you can share all this with! I actually adore you, Joan. I really, really do. You've got to believe me. I would never hurt you." I knew I shouldn't reveal myself, but I wanted to, so I did. "You do not need to be scared around me, Joan. I genuinely want to help."

Sitting in abject misery, Joan ordered me to head for home, and while I drove us back down Route 1, she writhed with unhappiness. She said, "So, who exactly have you told about me?"

"Joan, really, sweetie, we should not keep doing this."

"Eliza and Bernie's a given. But who else? Your mother?"

"Joan, I can't do this with you. I do talk to people close to me. But that's healthy, right?"

"So what have you told her?"

"I refuse to do this. It's completely sick."

"About my screwed-up family?"

"Joan, you have to accept that people talk and share independent of you. It's how we all make sense of our lives. It shouldn't have any bearing on how you think about yourself."

"And . . . about Gujie?"

"Joan, look. Like I said, I'm really pretty out of my mind over you, and I do talk about you a lot. But why is this like an addiction for you? Knowing all the specifics? Why are you so sure people are saying awful things?"

"Wow. Now I'm assuming you told her I tried to seduce my best friend's husband. So how about our first date—like that 'talk dirty to me' stuff?"

"This is none of your business."

"Wait a minute, you actually told your mother that I asked you to talk dirty?"

"Joan, I'm not going there."

It took Joan awhile to recover her voice. But when she did, she unleashed quite a torrent, doing her best to hurt. For the next hour in the car Joan assaulted every contour of my inadequacy. I was a fucking momma's-boy chump, I refused to see it, and it was time I saw it. And because she had a point, and because I sort of couldn't believe I'd told my mother these things, and because I actually did want my life to stop being like this, I listened. And the more I listened, the more I felt as though Joan might actually be ripping a veil from my eyes, exposing my inner life for the horror show it apparently was. She was a prophet of ugly truths, it seemed, and she spoke it all aloud because she was tortured by her horrible insights. She was damaged, she admitted, by what life had put her through, but at least she was a good and true soul who never stabbed friends in the back the way Eliza and I did, wasn't the phony I was, knew, unlike me, that nobody gave enough of a shit to be interested in her thoughts. While she was born with this knowledge, Eliza and I needed it all explained. And these were truths that, in order to be with her in any capacity whatsoever—even just to be her occasional lover—I needed to understand, along with the fact that, however much pain this was causing, her observations actually constituted a truer, deeper regard than I'd probably ever gotten before, because they depended on such an intimate knowledge of me. The only other choice I had, apparently, was to go back into the sleepwalking life of amoral blindness in which I'd passed the days before I met her. And the more I listened, the more I thought she was right. Her outrage, after all, was not the normal stuff of my life, so perhaps I had known only idiots until now, "enablers" who had failed to reflect my true self back at me. Perhaps I really was a weak monster in a morally righteous universe, my whole prior life an irrelevancy, and perhaps the future—if I really wanted to hold on to the miraculous Joan Artois—really would be an excruciating process of self-betterment.

When I stopped for gas, though, I felt like such dogshit that I couldn't imagine having the energy for all that self-betterment. I could only imagine sleeping and crying a lot, and because I'd been in relationships that involved a lot of sleeping and crying, I wanted most of all to just make peace, make a little love later on, and say good-bye in the morning. Joan, meanwhile, was wandering over to an upscale Victorian hotel and scanning the dinner menu. I could not afford to keep feeding Joan like this, but I also could not afford more misery. I was clearly much more pathetic than I'd ever known, and I was clearly in the company of the one woman who'd ever been able to show me, and I was glad for that. So I pleaded for the opportunity to buy her dinner, and we sat at a corner table, and I told myself I wasn't obsessed, I was just falling headlong out-of-my-gourd in love with an exquisitely complex and insightful woman, and had to accept that the love would go nowhere, and that it was just as well. Even if she was holding out the possibility that she might one day approve of me, and even be fond of me.

The room was warm enough, and the Friday night crowd was awfully genial, weekending couples sipping wine and playing footsie, but I was already drawing myself away, licking my wounds. Smells of seared meat and butter and garlic filled the room, and conversation rippled around the other tables—well-to-do spouses leaned close, some bored and others elated, enjoying money and free time in a pretty place. Our candle beam flickered across our dishes, and suddenly Joan kissed me without regard to audience. She wanted to put the fight behind us. She wanted to drink wine and forget about it and enjoy the night. She wanted to be lovers again. And I loved being lovers with her. Oh God, how I loved it. But then, while watching me order a hamburger—to her steak tartar—she said, "So why exactly are you worried about money all the time?"

"Broke. Nothing but a TA-ship."

"Really?"

"Yep. No trust fund, no nothing." I laughed. "Which is why you're right not to get involved with me."

She nodded.

"In fact, it's also why I'm thinking about a lot of different possibilities."

"Right."

"Directions I could go in, and that sort of thing."

She sighed and looked away. "I am such a child about money."

"Yeah?"

"I always assume there's going to be piles of it, forever. Millions. And I never even think about where it'll come from." She squinted across the room, then stepped over to sit in my lap. She wagged her head like a kid making a tough choice. "Hey, tell me what's going to happen when I'm living back here. And I don't mean with us. Just with me. Am I going to go over to my dad's house sometimes and hang out? Like a normal person?"

"Of course. But what do you think of this law school idea? Lot of years, to apply and get through and all that."

"Not if it's what you want."

"You think?"

"Of course."

"It doesn't sound like a bad choice to you?"

"Why do I get the feeling you're asking what I'm willing to settle for?"

Huh?

Joan kissed me again and said, "You're just incorrigible. You need to promise you won't call for a few days, okay? After I leave for New York?"

"Really?"

"I want you to promise you're coming, but I also want you to promise not to call." Kissing me one more time, she whispered, "And hey, do you know that I am so ready for bed?"

"The van's outside. Crawl into my sleeping bag and I'll get the check."

"Oh . . . but don't you wish we could walk right upstairs and slide between the sheets?" She kissed me again, and before our desserts and dessert wines made it to the table, I got a room key to have a look. Up the creaking mahogany stairs, and down a musty and squeaking hall, we entered the Captain Somebody-or-other suite, with its frilly white linens on a four-poster bed. An antique ice chest made a dresser against one wall, and I asked Joan if she could ever live in California again. She ignored me and walked over to a window, catching the moon's white warble on a black sea. I was looking for a card with the room rate when

Joan pulled her shirt off. I thought of closing the door—we hadn't paid yet—but she unhooked her bra, loosened her jeans. Hopping under the covers with a laugh, Joan asked, "What?"

"You're fantastic." And she was. She was a miracle, in her way.

"Come here."

"Shouldn't we pay?"

"Have me first."

"But, Joan, really, they could come up here, and we haven't paid for dinner either. They're going to freak out."

"We need to work on you, don't we? It's our last night together and you're worried about getting caught by the maid. But go ahead. Be a good boy, and if it makes you feel better, you can get my wallet from the car and charge my Visa. And buy some condoms while you're at it. I've got to be more careful."

Joan had ordered an Armagnac, at fourteen dollars a glass, so I stopped first in the dining room to down it between bites of her crème brûlée. I might be a rube, but that didn't mean I should waste my Porto and blackberry crisp, either. I really did love blackberries. And then I was pushing open the hotel's front door and taking my first breath of the cool maritime night, the seaweed and fish and evergreen smells. But I stopped yet again. Joan had indeed told me to get her wallet, and yes, we owed a crazy amount of money for that dinner, but she'd long since made it clear that she expected a man to take care of things. Which was what you missed growing up the way I had: Sex-Money-Power. And even if I really should be all over this, and dropping all feeling for this unstable girl, I should also avert my eyes yet again from the bill and open my forest-green Velcro wallet and pay for both dinner and room—roughly half my rent. So I did, knowing it would get me through this final time with Joan intact, and then I felt a surge of buyer's regret along with this weird rush of rightness and confidence, and then I bounded back upstairs. Running down the hallway, I reached for the Captain-Somebody-or-other doorknob and froze. I had almost forgotten the condoms, and I headed back down the stairs thinking, *Oh gee, Joan, let's add up my bumbles thus far—limpness, premature ejaculation, withheld ejaculation, momma's-boy incestuousness, forgetting rubbers.* Not much of a sexy leading man, after all. Not much of a Cary Grant. *But look forward,* I told myself, stepping into the seaside night. *Look forward and focus.*

The rain had stopped again and the streets gleamed wet. In the absence of cars or humming power lines, I heard the sound of slapping waves washed over the bluff-top meadows invisible now in the dark distance, over the shadowy wooden fences and onto the dim asphalt of the street. To the west, where I remembered there once being a head shop and used-book store, I found only art galleries with more wire-legged wooden seagulls in their darkened windows. Turning east, I passed one closed storefront after another and noticed an outlet from San Francisco's famously expensive Wilkes Bashford, haberdasher to the super-rich. Gujie and the Professor Sigmund character, the one Joan lived with in Europe, they probably both wore great suits. Especially in New York. Joan probably had great clothes, too, waiting for her in that New York closet. Nothing wrong with great clothes. The grocery store had to be open. Except it wasn't—closed at eight. Twenty-five minutes now since Joan beckoned, and I couldn't think of anywhere else to look. Jogging to Route 1, sweating and worried, I looked around for what I knew I wouldn't find: a convenience store, a gas station minimart. Standing beside the two-lane highway, I saw that I was beaten—nothing but asphalt and forest. And then I had a thought. Sprinting now, I darted past a gussied-up bed-and-breakfast, a jewelry shop's empty windows, an old water tank ghostly white atop its tower. Saturn and Venus twinkled like twin diamonds in the silver ring of the half-moon, and at the hotel saloon I quietly asked for help. Then I bolted, wheezing and sweating, up those mahogany stairs and down the hall.

"Oh shit," Joan asked later, "what's this?"

"It's all I could get."

"What the hell is it?"

"It's a Rough Rider."

"Are you out of your mind?"

"It's all I could get, Joan."

So she brought me inside, anyway, pantomiming tenderness, until I stopped.

"What?" she asked. "What are you doing?"

I thought the condom had torn. But again, I refused to apologize.

She shoved me away and dropped to the wood floor. Lying on her stomach, she folded her arms beneath her chest. I could hear waves crashing outside, and Joan muttered something about my sexual incompetence. After a while, she made the gesture I knew she would, pulling on a finger to bring me down, atop her back. She winced at my weight and the pain of her pelvic bones on the hard wood floor, her eyes wide open and worried in the pale glow. Joan had an authentic gift for a particular part of sex, and in a room lit with starlight she mouthed a delicious penance, dispensing an ambrosia she knew that she alone possessed. We lay awake a long time afterward, watching each other, and when I closed my eyes again I heard Joan whisper, "You are an awfully beautiful surfer boy, Cashie. You really are. It's been fun knowing you."

In my campus mailbox, I found the latest *New Yorker* magazine, a book called *The Naked Civil Servant* by Quentin Crisp, which I'd ordered at Joan's suggestion, and an annoyed note from my advisor, paper-clipped to an announcement for an adjunct freshman-comp position at U.C. Irvine— eighteen grand a year for two years, with a chance of renewal. Which was all very nice, but then what? Two years somewhere else at twenty? Maybe an assistant professorship in the hinterlands? My advisor's note said he'd contacted his friend and sent a letter of recommendation, ". . . and why couldn't you do me the courtesy of applying?" I sat down on the linoleum and looked around at the lecture announcements and mailboxes, the copy machine and the stapling table. And I saw what I could not stop myself from seeing: Joan in my bed, Joan in her bed, Joan on the beach and in my car, and most of all in New York. Joan's hair, Joan's mouth, Joan's bare back. I tried to visualize her apartment, working from movies set in New York, books I'd read, Edith Wharton. I'd visited a girl in New York a few times in college, and I reached for scraps: that street near N.Y.U. with the incredibly old little houses, where Henry James lived. The view of the park from the girl's family apartment, the building where John Lennon had lived. I was nineteen, and Lennon mattered to me. I remembered density, too: density of steel, stone, noise, light, flavor, texture, talk, and life. But if Joan asked again for me to come, I should probably decline. I knew this. I didn't feel it—in fact, I badly wanted to see her, and to go wherever our affair was meant to go—but I also felt increasingly lucky to have escaped her with my sanity. I felt lucky to have squeaked through test after test about my ability to keep my heart to myself, and I wasn't sure I could take such a colossal test: alone with her, just the two of us, in a faraway city. I liked the vision, of course—there was great sex appeal in the thought of a week in Manhattan with such a lovely and nutty woman. But also real anxiety. What if I came unglued? What if I blew it and told her I was falling in love with her? She'd eat me alive and chew me up and spit me out her high-rise window, and then I'd feel like shit and never see her again and forever carry the knowledge that I was simply not man enough for women like Joan Artois. Joan had even said not to call for a while, and what could that really mean except that there was another guy? Or two? Or three? Right now, all at once, in her bed? And I'd done a fine job of being Mr. Cool. I'd done okay. Not immaculate, not triumphant, but passing. At some point I had to say enough was enough, you've passed your exams, time to move on. Although it was still possible that Joan didn't realize I was in love with her, and that if she did, it would make a difference. Just like with her parents. If she'd only accept the fact that they loved her, and had screwed up, and wanted to be in her life, everything would probably be fine. I wanted to tell her to get over it, already. At some point, you're your own creation. You got to stop blaming people. The blame doesn't help, anyway. You're still fucked up, and you've still got to get un-fucked-up. I wanted to get un-fucked-up myself. Badly. I wondered what that would be like, being a little more together on the inside. I had no power over my own heart, and I had to acquire it. Because I would have to stop being the kind of turkey who tells his mother everything and falls head over heels for the wrong women and drives them away because he can't keep his heart to himself. If Joan knew that I was in love with her, she'd confess that she felt the same way, and that such feelings were incredibly rare between two people, and that we should set aside everything else in our lives and make those feelings grow.

I wondered if she'd have a lot of mementos of Gujie—pictures, gifts, the odd book. She'd be packing them all up, I supposed, trying to move on. She really did need to move on. The guy was no good. Rich, well-bred, whatever. But no good. He'd been a real bastard to her, and I would be kind. Although Joan's whole story was deeply suspicious. Too little agency on her part. Too poor a rendition of her own lunatic character. It didn't add up. With me, the story would have to add up. She'd force me to see my own illusions, but I'd also make her forgive her parents and take responsibility for the woman she'd become, and then we'd love each other right. We'd have relentless dirty sex and tell each other everything and feel safe with each other. Except we wouldn't. Because she didn't want that. She just wanted the sex, and the talking, and the joy; she didn't want the mutual-attachment part. And that really should be fine with me. If I were strong, that would be fine. But I was no longer sure how strong I was. I wished I could be with Joan right now, to help. I thought of calling again, just to tell her, Hey, I'm available to help. Just concerned about you, that's all. But I also wished my most recent voice mail had not been so aggressive: "How about giving me a call, huh?" Probably put her off. Joan hated pushiness. She hated my pushiness in particular. But I had to start pushing. I couldn't live in limbo with her. I had to ask for what I wanted, and walk away if I couldn't get it. Still, she might be withholding her return phone call in order to give me time for reflection. Despite the fact that she was moving home, she'd made it clear that she was not interested in commitment. She was being kind, in that way. Letting me get there myself. Trusting me to see that my fantasies of a big future were just that, fantasies. But Joan had also yanked some plug in my heart, and my most vital emotional fluids were gurgling out. I wanted to call her and tell her to put the plug back in. How could she ignore me like this? How could she make love with such blissful abandon and tell me all about her life and then vanish? Well, because she had her own sadness to solve, her own wounds to nurse. That was the rub. That was the part I had to be man enough to accept. She also knew that I sucked, of course, but I had to accept that, too, at some level. I wanted to call and tell her I accepted that. I know I suck, Joan. I fucking hate myself. And it's helping me a lot. I'm really going to grow and change and become a stronger person. Which will really help me support you better. It's all starting to happen for me. I'm going to do it myself, too. You don't have to do it for me. I'm not asking you to tell me I'm okay anymore. I'm telling myself now. It's really helping me understand my whole stupid romantic history, and how it's always been my fault, and how my grandfather's distaste for me and my father has to do with what needy pussies we both are. My father was a fantastic guy, the best a kid could ever want, but on the phone recently I'd started understanding that tremor in his self-confidence. Rambling about a corporate attorney named Agertelis, my father had said, "Remember him? Very good lawyer, I mean *scary* good, one of these Harvard Law School guys whose brain just *works*. He's like a laser. He was a full partner: two hundred K a year, condo at Alpine, kid at Yale, and I was down at the courthouse yesterday and Agertelis was out there in the hallway and they fired him. Twenty years, and the other partners just decided one day, That's it. He's out. And the next thing he knows, his wife's divorcing him and keeping the house. And you know what? He's happier than he's ever been. He's saying, 'Jack, you got to show me all this stuff you do. The music and the Zen. I'm getting back to what matters.' He said, 'Jack, I'm fifty-five years old, I've worked every day of my life, I'm out. I'm not doing this anymore.' He filed for bankruptcy, and he's moving up to Sonoma, and he's starting a little fruitstand on the highway next to a rich buddy's winery, and somehow it made me so glad." For the first time in my life, I'd heard the way my father looked to others for validation, and I resolved that I would no longer do the same. I heard all the worry behind his inspirational tale: *Wasn't I actually a fool to chase dreams over security? Couldn't I really have been someone else? Walked some other road to a safer place? Or is the specificity of character—the immutable nature of who we are—somehow inescapable? Can't I please feel that the life I led was the only good life I could have led, given who I was? A necessary kind of destiny?* Sitting still on the mail-room floor, my blood pumping with the fear of similar traps I might already be setting myself, traps that would render me unfit for the affections of the discriminating and demanding Joan Artois, I thought what sons have thought at such moments from time immemorial: *Fuck the relentless, defensive assertion that life isn't lived in your wallet or the size of your retirement account, but rather in the thoughts you made time to think—banal old distinctions, anyway, flattening life into goods and bads, clean rights and wrongs, the decent people and the profane. Fuck all this acceptance of limitations, self-reinvention need not apply. What about protection against hard times? What about victory?* The truth was that my father had always provided just fine, better than fine, but maybe he was losing confidence because he'd kept his head in the sand of his own idealism all these years, failed to see what you'd want on the back end of life, and what if academia was my own little escapist sandbox? Hadn't I also seen Mom glancing over to my father during our last family dinner and thought to myself, *Oh no, see. This is exactly what I never want a woman to feel upon looking at me. The quiet disrespect that wears you down, crushes you, takes away your strength—right there in Mom's face, in these spasms of Kabuki-like, stylized nausea as my father again rubs his dry eyes. Not that she doesn't love him to death, because she does. And not that she doesn't respect and treasure him at some deeper level, because that's there, too. But maybe I've got to hold it together better than that entire scene, keep my head screwed on. Press my shirts and learn not to pick my nose or talk while chewing or expect anyone to like me, and most of all, I've got to make a little goddamn money, because it's the only guarantor of dignity.*

Except, see, the point was not to call Joan. The point was to forget about her.

Rubbing my face now, shaking my face, I blinked a few times and tried to clear my mind. This navel-gazing self-loathing was clearly half the problem. Not the whole problem—because I was indeed unwittingly manipulative and caught in childhood psychology—but fully half the problem for sure. If not more. Which was why I should look carefully at this proposed New York trip. Caution was almost certainly the better part of valor. I was still sitting on the mail-room floor—dirty linoleum, other grad students coming and going and occasionally nodding at me. I smelled terrible. Coffee always gave me body odor. I flipped through my *New Yorker* and saw nothing but Joan: first in Gore Vidal's memory of the late Clare Boothe Luce, born impoverished and illegitimate to a mother who'd started out as a call girl and ended as a kept woman. Luce had married a series of extremely wealthy men who each passed a bit along to her—including *Time* magazine founder Henry Luce—and she'd worked at *Vogue* before managing *Vanity Fair* and becoming a successful playwright. Later in life, she "swam, snorkeled, water-skied; and outlived most of her detractors, while occasionally dropping a bit of acid." She was, in Vidal's view, "easily the most hated woman of her time—she was too beautiful, too successful in the theatre, in politics, in marriage." Another article profiled a woman "so unnervingly beautiful that ugliness of all sorts falls to pieces around her." Raised by her mother to be a beauty above all else, "Francine" had, in the course of her life, charmed Alfred Hitchcock, danced before Charlie Chaplin (and won his flattery), and jitterbugged to "Blue Suede Shoes" with Elvis himself. Francine's greatest beauty lay beneath her skin—a grace that followed her around, a function of her knowledge that there would always be another man to take care of her. This created a kind of halo effect in which men "acted as though being around her for a while could free them of being too shallow, too ugly, too stupid, too rich, not rich enough, too high-minded, too preoccupied with business or television or revenge or sexual fixation, or whatever they hated about themselves." And of course, this was all Joan, because of course she'd fucked the greatest and wealthiest men in the greatest hotels in the world— Italian heirs and French aristocrats and Danish bodybuilders— and of course she'd had masterful anal sex with anal superheroes in Parisian penthouses, followed by lavish dinners at the world's finest restaurants as a deserved reward. She'd worn the finest lingerie, graced the finest resorts in both the snow and the tropics, and been made to come for weeks on end by both men and women, loving every goddamn minute of it and intending to do it all again, questioning only whether I was a worthy companion.

I looked at my phone, punched Joan's number, and felt a shudder of relief when she didn't answer. Francine, the beauty in the magazine, had married four times and received fourteen marriage proposals, including those from a Turkish aristocrat, a French marquis, the son of a Nazi officer, a Boston Brahmin, a stockbroker, an orthodontist, and heirs to an emerald mine in Colombia, a newspaper empire in Paris, a Texas oil fortune, the Dunlop-tires fortune, a pharmaceutical fortune, and a Southern grocery-store chain. "It really is one of my dirty little secrets," Joan had once said, "how many men have thought they were going to marry me."

"But is that true?" I'd asked. "Or is it bullshit?"

"I do not bullshit."

"Sorry."

"Not ever. That's your department."

I was staring at Shauna's mailbox. The little label said, SHAUNA ROSE. She was back from her trip, and I was supposed to see her that night, and I wished I could see her sooner. We'd make love and I'd feel better. I'd grow stronger by making love to Shauna. Unless I was honest with her. Because, boy, did she ever deserve honesty. I had to be honest with her. I had to tell her I was in love with someone else. Not that I was involved, or that it was going anywhere, because it was not. I might see her again, but that was all. And the real point was that my heart was a disaster area and Shauna should steer clear. Protect herself. I'd met Shauna right here, in fact: the cherubic scholar with the wide-set watery eyes, flipping through student papers. Most graduate students disliked me, for reasons I didn't understand, but I'd had a feeling about Shauna—her curly hair in a bun, faded jeans flattering, black T-shirt over magnanimous breasts. She'd been wearing suede cowboy boots, too, in a kind of guile-less, not-quite-up-to-date *frisson* of groovy earnestness that made me think we'd have a lot to say to each other.

"Hey there," I'd begun, with such promise, "you're Shauna, right?"

"Indeed." She'd been lost in thought, sorting mail.

"I'm Harper," I said. "We met a couple years ago, at Gary Sutter's place."

"Oh, right." She read an announcement for a lecture that evening: "Beowulf and the Body: The Poetics of Dismemberment," 242 Whalen Hall at 7:30.

"You on the job market this year?" I asked.

"Huh?" She glanced over. "Ah yes. I am."

"Did you go to the MLA?"

She nodded.

"I didn't even bother. It's too brutal. I mean, who needs it, if you're just going to watch other people get jobs?"

"I had fun, actually."

"Oh."

She nodded again, stepped away to look at an announcement on the bulletin board. Feigning curiosity, I followed her gaze: Professor Joey Recht, chair of the U.C. Santa Cruz doctoral program in the History of Consciousness, was offering a special seminar called "The Decline of the West as a Sexual Position."

"I heard him speak about *Playgirl*," Shauna said, "and why it was an economic failure. He argues that straight female desire just doesn't eroticize the violation of men—it's not built around the rapist role—so the magazine was like a photo album of well-oiled and very handsome flashers."

"Hey, you don't want to get lunch, do you? Right now?"

"No, I don't."

"You don't?"

"No."

"Right. Well, it was just a thought."

"Yeah."

"I mean, I was just hungry."

She stared at me, blank.

"And I was on my way up to Northside, and I thought,

you know, sometimes it's nice to talk to someone over a meal."

She nodded, finally focusing on what I was doing.

"Well, see you around, huh?"

She looked quizzical. Then she said, "Bye?"

That very evening, I was grading papers at my desk—just a junkyard door atop two cheap metal file cabinets—and I was listening to Joni Mitchell's seminal *Court and Spark*, when Shauna called, "Is Harper there?"

"Speaking."

"Shauna Rose here, from the English Department."

"Hi."

"Look, ah, tell me what you meant, in the mail room."

"By what?"

"By asking me to lunch."

"Oh hey, I'm sorry. I really understand. I was just, you know, looking for company, and . . ."

"And what?"

"Nothing at all. I promise. I didn't mean anything by it. I just, you know, it just popped out of my mouth, and . . ."

"Oh."

"Yeah."

"Well, anyway."

"Wait, why do you ask?"

"Oh . . ."

"Really, tell me."

"Oh boy. This is going to sound ridiculous, but I just wanted to know if it was me you wanted to have lunch with, or just anybody. Because if it was me specifically, and, you know . . . because . . . we could have lunch another time. Assuming that's what you meant."

And see, I *loved* this kind of talk. I knew exactly who I was with this kind of talk. If I could only get myself done with this dating-around phase, this certainty that I needed to experience something I had not yet experienced—and harden myself in some way I was manifestly unhard—I would embrace this kind of talk. I called Shauna, didn't get through, and marched down a hallway full of students and shuffling professors toward her office. Maybe she had office hours. It'd be nice to hang out with her, pass some time. What if I blew it? What if I saw Joan yet again, and got all wrapped up in her lunacy, and lost Shauna, and then it turned out Shauna was the girl for me? Well, that would stink. Which is why I needed to get this Joan business out of my system. Maybe Shauna and I could have a few drinks tonight, and not even make love. Maybe I could feign exhaustion and go home early. Obsession feels terrible. People talk about obsession like it's this great thing. They smile when they talk about their obsessions. *I'm so obsessed with golf! I practice putting in my office! Isn't that hilarious!* But those people aren't actually obsessive. Obsessive people enjoy their obsessions only when they're young. Later, they realize that obsession is ruining their life.

How's this for a contrast in first dates: Joan at the Cliff House, being Lady Bizarro, and Shauna at a Thai barbecue place, talking shop over the baby back ribs—my bigoted pro-slavery novelists, her long-neglected female Renaissance poet's daringly subversive feminist critique. "They let *you* teach Race, Class, Gender, and Sexuality?" she'd asked. "But you have none of those things." She'd arrived looking more bookish than I recalled, in reading glasses and a tweed sport coat, but while rain banged off the restaurant windows the coat came off to reveal a little tank-top thing, and her bare shoulders sort of shivered. Lunch drifted to coffee, coffee to a walk under my umbrella, and by the time the sun set gold in a clearing purple sky Shauna and I were not at each other's throats but were rather back at that woodsy cottage and well on our way to one of those endless first dates during which a long-term relationship seems a foregone conclusion. So what the hell was I doing now? Although I'd wondered from the start if our connection didn't come too easily, was it really so crazy to want a dragon at the castle gate, piles of armor-clad skeletons from the legions of failed suitors? But why think less of her for not judging me a sociopathic creep? Even if I *was* a little bit of a sociopathic creep? Why dislike her for celebrating my good qualities? For insisting that I had a decent heart, and that I was a pleasing lover and a funny dancer?

Shauna had made couscous and vegetables that first night, and we'd sat on her futon couch and talked also about how we both played Dungeons and Dragons as kids, and she'd always had powerful ranger-cleric characters. She'd been a nerd. Me too. Shauna had an acoustic guitar, and a lot of songbooks tucked into shelves, and I told her that I did, too. After the whole heavy-metal-genocide phase, during my Vicky blues, I'd joyously embraced my father's music, swapping bluegrass licks with his five-string banjo. I'd learned a lot of Crosby Stills & Nash, too, and Neil Young. The good obvious stuff. Shauna's shelves also carried Judith Butler's *Gender Trouble* and Certeau's *The Practice of Everyday Life*, as well as a complete library of Renaissance classics. In this way, we were different: my shelves were all Whitman and Emerson, histories of the Civil War. She told me about her tall and handsome father dying in a plane crash when she was ten—still the salient emotional fact of Shauna's life. She'd kept his pipe collection, secretly carried one around so she could always sneak a smell and be reminded. Her newly widowed mother, Shauna told me, "a mythical Medusa," decided to kill her children and herself, but was saved by a 1970s consciousness-raising group that got her back into college and into sexual experimentation with the young teacher on whom Shauna, too, had a crush. Herself the young Electra, as Shauna put it—compulsively thinking in myth—she had lived too much of her life in revenge, even getting her own dope-smoking, poetry-writing boyfriend with whom to have adolescent sex in the afternoons. "And boy oh boy," Shauna told me with embarrassment, having invited me up the ladder to that loft for the first time, fading umber light on her pretty eyes, "do you ever look just like that guy." The date even ended well, Shauna sending me off to sleep at home. "Not because I have anything to do in the morning," she said. "I'm just feeling, I don't know, sort of . . . saturated. Saturated with Harper. Is that okay?"

In a campus coffeeshop, quite near Shauna's office, I started flipping through that book, *The Naked Civil Servant*. It was a classic of gay male narrative, topping every such reading list, and Joan loved it. She said she'd always felt like a gay man trapped in a woman's body. Sort of a hackneyed joke, but Joan seemed not to know that. Sometimes she was ironic and knowing; sometimes she was not. I bought a cup of coffee, started sweating again, and began to read: "As soon as I stepped out of my mother's womb," Crisp writes, "I knew I had made a mistake." Vintage Joan, of course, as was Crisp's declaring himself an unwanted child from the very beginning, and his tale of catching pneumonia when only a few days old. So delicious does he find the ensuing monopoly on his mother's attention that he spends the next twelve years repeating the trick by crying or playing sick or wetting or soiling himself, and while his mother occasionally scolds or punishes him as she cleans yet again his stinking knickers, "I never really felt guilty," Crisp recalls. "I thought my vomit, my feces, my tears were love gifts to my mother—no more disgusting, after all, than a broken heart." But what else rang so true for Joan? Parental indifference leading to Crisp's abduction and (implied) sodomization by a "rag and bone man"? His confession to an "inordinate lust for praise"? Throughout his childhood, Crisp writes, he played with girls because boys only wanted to fight, while girls could be bullied (with shouts or punches) into dressing up in someone's mother's cast-off finery and fantasizing to the effect that, "This wheelbarrow is my carriage. I gather up my train as I get in. Get in the other side, you fool. I nod to the servants as I leave. No. I ignore them. I am very proud and very beautiful." As a boarding-school student, Crisp confesses, he wanted most of all "to use sex as a weapon to allure, subjugate, and, if possible, destroy the personality of others." Thus, Crisp writes, he was always more interested in the schoolmasters than in his classmates, and he worked endlessly at seducing them, forfeiting all friendship with boys his own age. Likewise, Crisp's view of prostitution: whereas the average woman saw loving and being loved as normal, believing a man when he said that he loved her, Crisp explains that a homosexual, toward whom most advances were at best insincere, at worst hostile, saw real affection as requiring proof, and "What better proof," Crisp asks rhetorically, "than money?"

I'd been wrong about my sexuality. I'd thought I was a pro, and I was not a pro. I was a kid. I'd thought I was a real Satan in the sack, and I was a choirboy. Joan had had much better sex than I could give. But here, too, I could perhaps hang on long enough to learn. I could perhaps apply myself. I could grow and prove to her that I'd grown. I picked up an *East Bay Express*, and dialed a sex line, looking for help from a dirty-talking pro. Right off, while I stepped back into the sunshine, for a little privacy on my cell, I got a sultry young woman who claimed to be in Sherman Oaks, California.

"I really need some help," I told her.

"That's what I'm here for, baby."

"Not like that. I need to learn how to talk dirty. Right now.

Like what a woman really wants to hear when she says, 'Talk dirty to me.' "

"You want me to talk dirty to you?"

"No. Really. I just want to know what a woman wants to hear."

"Mm . . . well, girls mostly want to hear stuff like 'You like it hard, don't you? You horny li'l bitch. Yeah, I'm going to slap your ass, you dirty slut.' "

"You're serious."

"Not just slutty girls, either, but real respectable-type grown-up ladies."

Like Joan.

"And they *do* want you to spank 'em, for real."

This much I did know, because Joan loved to be spanked. She'd had to coach me, giving instructions over her shoulder, telling me how hard. I had no intuitive feel for these things.

Phone-Sex Lady said, "So you like that, baby?"

"What?"

"Talking about spanking. Are you turned on right now?"

Maybe.

"You want to spank me now, don't you?"

"Ah . . . I'm not sure."

"Or . . . you know, I been thinking I'm not acting right, and . . ."

But it wasn't me I needed to understand, it was Joan. Phone-Sex Lady was all about men. She was an expert at figuring out what a man wanted to think certain kinds of women wanted to hear. And that wasn't the point. I needed to know what women *actually* wanted to hear. So I flipped around some more in the *Guardian*, looking for a women-oriented sex line. Then I dialed a few. Immediately, I discovered something interesting: every single one connected you to a soothing and prerecorded female *ur*-voice, instead of a live operator. Where men, apparently, just wanted a living, breathing female to say, "Okay, you want me to blow you, baby? Here I go, I'm blowing you, oh God, your cock is so giant," the porn industry had apparently concluded that women wanted . . . what? This sugar-sweet and not-exactly-living soul sister to help them shed their inhibitions and discover what really excites them. Where did that leave me? In fact, as one of these women's line continued, I realized there were no live humans anywhere in the system. Nothing but "true confessions" services, in which you listened to the recorded confessions of anonymous others, then recorded your own, and apparently got some big thrill out of imagining what strangers would think; and touch-tone menus of prerecorded audio fantasies: "If bare round bottoms and over the knees spankies exist in your fantasies, press 1." The next menu began, "For 'Sweet discipline,' press 1. For 'Hanky-spanky,' press 2. For 'Naughty girls,' press 3." Well, naturally, I pressed 3, and heard one woman saying to another. "Gee, Amy, isn't it fun having a twin sister to play with when your husband's not home?" Soon the girls had gotten into Phillip's best cigars and finest wines, certain he wouldn't be home for hours. But then: what's that noise? A door opening! "Amy? Are you home? Hey, what's that smell . . . Amy, what have I told you about getting into my cigars? You've been a very naughty girl, and you know what happens to naughty girls, don't you?"

"We won't do it again, we promise!"

"I know you won't, because I'm going to give you a spanking you won't soon forget, and Amy knows how much I like to spank naughty girls."

"Please give us one more chance."

"I'm afraid not. Amy, come over here and lift your skirt while I pull your white panties down and spank your little behind. Oh, Amy, you like to be spanked, don't you?"

"Yeah!" she whines happily.

"You want it harder, don't you?"

"Yeah, I *do*!"

"Now tell your sister what I do after I spank you! Tell her!"

The only person in Shauna's office, unfortunately, was the guy with whom she shared it, a nervous Derridean who'd been born without a urethra and suffered years of penile reconstructive surgery—shredded Levi's, shaggy hair over his face, Converse Chuck Taylors—and only halfway through graduate school emerged from yet another scalpel-session with such beauty that he'd finally felt empowered to lose his virginity. And all of a sudden the guy looked great, skin clear and hair short, slick new personal style of black turtleneck, black slacks, and clunky black shoes, even an expensive new black briefcase. He promised to tell Shauna I was looking for her, and that I was in a lecture at Barrows Hall but that I'd be free all afternoon.

Dean Reynolds had titled her Monday lecture "Coon, Cohen, Cunt: The Geometry of Prejudice," and while I thought about Joan in far-off New York, I moved strongly toward the idea that I should not go to New York, even if she asked. The dean made a lot of notes on the chalkboard: Frankfurt School neo-Marxist critique of positivism, poststructuralism growing inevitably out of structuralism, postmodernism with a big question mark after it, the word "ethics" underlined three times. And of course the real reason I should probably rethink my career was that my mind was always too full of emotional drama to hold high theory for more than about ten minutes. Show me Lyotard's hugely important *The Postmodern Condition*—casual toilet reading for a gal like Shauna, who would doubtless be sweet that afternoon, with a two-timing asshole who was somehow going to muster the courage to be honest—and all I could do was navel-gaze about the necessary conditions for romantic fulfillment.

The dean, who offered that day to buy lunch for her instructors, was a great woman, simultaneously radical and moderate, maternal and intellectually rigorous. Walking behind her on teeming Telegraph Avenue, while she led us all to a restaurant, picking our way past tie-dyed T-shirt stands and incense vendors and steel-drum players, I yearned to radiate the dean's air of having been to the bottom of herself, seen the worst, and reassembled an enjoyable life. With all of us TAs—including the ones I called Guamanian-Literature Woman and Therapy Guy, both friends of Shauna's—the dean sat at a big wooden table in an English-pub-style sports bar and began a discussion of a new Foucault biography, how Foucault thought there was no inner essence to our sexual nature, only culturally fabricated fictions perpetrated by state institutions in order to control people's bodies and the pleasures those bodies could feel. Foucault was a giant, a backbone of contemporary criticism. And because I couldn't think of anything smart to say, and because I was the kind of narcissist who couldn't bear not to join a discussion, I told everyone about a poet I'd liked in college: He came into class and asked if we'd ever thought any truly inexcusable thoughts, and all us undergrads blushed, so the poet said, "Well, I have. Just this morning the quote of the day in *The Dartmouth* was 'The intellect is neither black nor white, it is color-blind.' " Really enjoying the anecdote, I said that the poet paused, looked around at all us kids, and said, "I thought to myself, That can't be true, because cum is white."

The table was silent, everyone dumbstruck.

Therapy Guy was so offended that he glanced outside, to the students on the street.

The others carried on like nothing had happened, which was nice of them—dipping onion rings in blue-cheese dressing and talking about President Clinton.

Only Joan could restore my self-regard. Insane, on the face

of it. Stupid. I was over that kind of thinking for good. My self-regard, I now declared, was my own charge. Nobody could take that away from me. Joan's emotional radar did have a dazzling accuracy, though.

Lunch arrived, big spinach salads and barbecued-beef sandwiches, and I tried my best to participate in the faculty conversation, which centered as usual on the difficulty of getting our racist, privileged students to realize just how racist and privileged they were. "They still don't get it," said a constitutionally exasperated blond woman with brass bangles, theorizing now that it would require a "white, most-likely heterosexual, presumably of Wasp background, male" to take the challenge and make this tectonic social change a reality. Everyone looked at me, but before I could accept their draft, the woman's pretty little daughter, drawing pictures and occasionally shrieking gibberish to shut up her mother, told me she was born six weeks early on a full moon complete lunar eclipse at midnight. "Guess how much I weighed," she demanded proudly.

"Four pounds?" I asked.

"Nope."

"Less?"

"Guilt!" she screamed suddenly. "Guilt! Guilt! Guilt!"

The girl's mother stopped whatever she'd been saying and the faculty talk went elsewhere, and I asked the girl, "You weighed less than four pounds?"

"Uh-huh," she replied.

"Three?"

"Two. Guess how much I weigh now."

"Don't know."

"Sixty pounds."

"Is that little for a ten-year-old?"

"Yes, it is. My friend Lani's ten and she weighs one-ten."

She drew me a castle and asked me what it was.

"A castle?"

"But what kind?"

"I don't know."

"A *floating* castle. See, there's floating ones and there's flying ones and other ones, too."

"Oh."

"Now you draw something," she said, handing me a crayon.

For lack of a better idea, I drew her a .357 Magnum, which she liked. Then I drew an ICBM and realized what I was doing and walked out to the sidewalk to use my cell phone. Tell Joan it was off. Tell her I wasn't coming. *How's New York? Settling in? Oh yeah, you know I think I probably shouldn't visit.* Students shuffled up and down the street, bags full of books, and a shaggy young man with an electric guitar sang about the Lord Jesus Christ. A large crowd listened closely, and another lost soul, in a polka-dotted jumpsuit, lay flat on his back, on the sidewalk, reeling in the sky. I cooled my voice, very calm. I pictured a Manhattan street, the cell phone in her bag. Or pocket. More likely her pocket.

And then my phone buzzed.

"Harp, baby. It's me, Joan."

"Oh hey, what a surprise? How are you?"

"Have I told you how much they overheat apartments in New York?"

Joan's voice rang inside me like a molecular authority, as if I'd known her all my life and *would* know her until I died. "Pretty hot, huh?"

"I feel like I'm withering up."

"Can't you turn down the heater?"

"Broke." She made a flapping noise with her mouth, as if bored. "I think I'm sick." She tore some kind of plastic wrap.

"Yeah, sick like what?"

She chewed something crunchy. "Mm . . . I just feel like, bleagh . . . can't concentrate, can't eat. Don't you even miss me? Aren't you at all curious about what I've been doing?"

"What have you been doing."

"Just stuff."

"What *kind* of stuff?"

"*Stuffy* stuff, I don't know. Do you think it's possible I'm getting some kind of bad electric juju from my vibrator?"

"What?"

"Like through the electrical wires, from using it too much?"

"How much have you been using it?"

"But do you think maybe you're not supposed to use them too much—like a microwave oven, or something—and that's what's making me sick?"

"How much have you been using it?"

"I don't know. A lot. I'm bored to death."

"What's a lot?"

"Just tell me what you think, if that's possible. About the electricity. It's so hot in here, and I don't have my furniture yet, so all I can do is lie around."

"Why don't you call the heat guy and cool down?"

"In my condition? I'd probably end up having sex with him."

"Lovely."

"Sorry."

"We're too far apart for that."

"What would you do if we weren't? Quick, right now."

"I would lick you and swallow you and digest you, and thus become you."

"Wow."

"You like?"

"I do."

We were silent a moment.

"Ooh . . . I wish . . ."

"You wish what?"

"That I had a million dollars." She laughed at herself. "No, I wish . . . I don't know. I wish I had more friends and a normal job and a normal life."

"Yeah? What else?"

"Well, I wish I were a mother."

"You do?"

"Sure. And a dog owner. And a homeowner. And . . . maybe I wish I had some growth spurts once in a while. That'd be nice. I wish I weren't so developmentally arrested, too, and maybe that I could shine more often in the areas that I do shine."

"And?"

"That I weren't so needy. And that I had more of a tan. And . . . do you know that I wish I were more airborne? I played basketball yesterday."

"That's funny."

"Yeah, airborne. It'd be nice to have fun things lined up to do all the time, too, and to have a little more to occupy my mind than my own problems sometimes, and . . ."

"Yeah?"

"Well, I'm wondering if you want to come to New York."

"Do you want me there?"

"Mmm-hmm."

"For real?"

"If you can keep your shit together, I do. I'm just bored and lonely, and it seems like a real pity."

I looked over at that little girl, doodling away. I saw her mother's eyes, their love and worry. "Can I think about it?"

"Not for too long. I might change my mind."

I turned off the phone and stepped back into the restaurant and waved at the dean and headed for the men's room. While I locked the door, my phone buzzed and I saw that it was Joan, but I didn't answer. I sat on the toilet, and then I got up and washed my face and the phone buzzed again. Again, I didn't answer. I dialed Shauna instead. I had to tell Shauna to stay away from me. But her voice mail kicked in, so I called Bernie at work. I told him that I'd betrayed his confidence to Joan, and that I was sorry, I was an asshole, and he told me to stop it. Relax, he said. Slow down. Then I told Bernie I was afraid of going to visit Joan. Something about her unmanned me, brought out the worst in me, even as it made me feel that I was finally living. I told him I'd never felt so exhilarated by a woman in my life, that I was pretty sure I was falling in love and that I knew she loved me, too, but that she could turn me off like a light. One minute, I'm her number one hero; the next, I'm a stranger. My phone's call waiting beeped—Joan yet again—but I told Bernie that no matter how badly we fought, I wanted her more. And I knew I had to crush that part of myself once and for all. The only problem was that Joan had this exquisitely clear vision of what a man was supposed to be, and I did not, and I wanted to, and maybe growing into her version was the only escape route from my own lameness. The only way to emerge as the impressive guy I'd always hoped to become. I said that being with Joan was like sticking my wet finger in the electric socket of my own unconscious. Thrilling and perhaps lethal. I wondered aloud if I should quit graduate school for something more lucrative—although money was only part of the picture. There was also this business of being completely "over" oneself. It was something Joan said frequently, about how the best men were "over themselves," which I thought meant freedom from ego and childhood guilt and emotional neediness, awareness of all one's worst psychological complexes, and also being evenly bisexual, a joyous bottom in gay sex and a cruel top in straight sex. Freedom from inhibition, too. Because nothing scared her sexually. It was as if she demanded flawless coherence of self and masterful delivery of anal sex—based on great experience receiving it. "It's funny," she'd once told me, "I started having anal sex to find out what it's like to be a man." And for some reason this was a flaw of mine. I was no good at it.

"Me neither," Bernie said.

My call waiting beeped again, and this time I flashed over to Joan. "What do you want?" I asked.

"I want my answer."

"I can't talk to you right now." I flashed back to Bernie and asked if he owned any stocks or bonds.

"You're watching the market?" he asked.

"Am I wrong, or is it maybe free money?"

"Do you know about the miracle of compound interest?"

"Tell me."

"I figured out that if I invest fifty bucks, and I realize a mere thirty percent annual return for the next thirty years . . ."

"Thirty percent?"

"Just hypothetically. But do you know how much money that would be? Fifty million dollars."

"Should I tell Shauna it's over? I'm going to see her in a few hours."

"Shauna's the keeper."

"So I shouldn't go to New York?"

"No, you should go to New York and have a great time, and come back and be with Shauna. That's what you should do."

"Do you know what the hell Joan's big objection is, though? To me? For why it all just has to be a fling?"

"It's better as a fling, Harp. It's a marvelous fling."

My call waiting beeped again. I flashed again. "Joan," I said, "what do you want?"

"Harper, my feelings are getting hurt."

I flashed back to Bernie, and he said, "Harp, she only really likes Guidos, anyway. You have to take this at face value. Go on her terms, or don't go at all."

I flashed back to Joan: "Tomorrow?"

"I would so love that."

Shauna liked me the way I was. She thought I was immature, and she knew better than to trust me (why did nobody trust me?), but she seemed to believe that I was a decent person. Which was confusing. The surfing, even—she loved my slipping out of bed at five in the morning, and she spoke glowingly about the comfy slumber of knowing her man was out conquering giant waves. She'd never had such a traditionally gendered love affair, she told me, and she exulted even in making me an egg burrito for the road, rousing herself in the darkness while I packed my wetsuit. And what of the lovely mornings in Berkeley, at her cottage? The weird pancakes she inexplicably deep-fried in canola oil or—much better, as a memory—the steam rising from her 1957 Airstream Griddle and Waffle Baker, light pouring through her multipaned windows with the front door open to the jasmine-scented breeze, partner-dancing to the great Julian Bream album *Romantic Guitar*.

"Hey there," I said, when Shauna finally answered her phone.

"What's up, baby?"

Ah . . . "What's up with you?"

"Well, I got a callback at N.Y.U. And I looked on the Web.

They've got an adjunct position in nineteenth-century American, in case you're interested."

Shauna was amazing.

"I'm flying out on Thursday. I'm going to see my mom again, too. She's getting me a father." Shauna chuckled.

"What?"

"My mother's getting married."

"To the guy you thought was physically repulsive?"

"I shouldn't have said that. God, I'm a bad person. Anyway, he offered to legally adopt me."

"But that's beautiful."

"Isn't it? I mean, it's sort of contrived, in a way."

"What else is there but contrived?"

"Right. I guess so. Yeah, I'm actually happy about it."

"He must be a decent man. Hey, where are you?"

"Home."

"Can I come over?"

"Meet me on Telegraph. I'm scared of you."

We noodled around town for an hour, Shauna wearing a brown leather jacket and her pointy cowboy boots. She kept glancing at me sideways, and she mentioned several times that I looked awful and that I should tell her what was wrong as soon as I felt ready. I said I would. I promised I would. Because I would. Soon. She wanted to shop for new eyeglasses, so I tagged along to a Telegraph Avenue boutique where the optometrist commented on Shauna's wide-set eyes—a desirable trait for eyeglass models, along with her narrow tapered chin and slender nose, the whole combination having been scientifically proven to be attractive in all human cultures. I asked if we could go back to her place now, but she stared at me and rumpled her nose and said, "But then we'll have sex. And you won't tell me whatever you're supposed to tell me." She wanted to get dinner first. On our way to a sushi place, Shauna said maybe she was tired of dating. "I'm not sure I have the stomach anymore. You know what I mean?" I knew perfectly. My own stomach was gone. No more stomach. Entering this little Japanese restaurant, and standing behind the bamboo screen by the register, I kept my breathing deep while Shauna haggled for a private table and then asked the waitress to turn down the lights and change the music. We had a big feed, with hot sake and raw anemone and eel. Then Shauna let me drive her little blue Porsche—though still not to her cottage. She wanted to meet a friend of hers, for dessert. "Remember," she said, "you promised we could go out with friends of mine. Like a normal couple."

The car was fantastic, and if we stayed together I'd get to drive it all the time. Although her steering pulled left. "I know," Shauna said, "I need the tires aligned, but it seems so incredibly symbolic, pulling to the left, like maybe I should see a faith healer instead of a mechanic. And you know, I got the most peculiar feeling on the way to see you today."

"Oh?"

"I was asking myself, 'What is this feeling? I know this feeling.' And then I realized: 'Oh yeah, I feel thirty.' "

"How does that feel?"

"Just very real. Neither the life of the party nor a boundaryless blob. Adult. It always happens when I see my mother, because she's so much the child, in a way. Are you sure you don't want to just come clean? And tell me the deal? If it's another woman, I can handle that. I just want to know where I stand."

Not only had Shauna never insinuated that I was anything but kind and harmless and perfect for her in particular, she'd tried surfing once and wanted to go again; she'd even read chapters of my dissertation and offered excellent advice. "Athletes of pleasure," she'd said of our first two weeks together. "I feel so dilated around you. A friend once asked if I'd rather have heart-felt fumbling or cold skill, and I said, 'Can't I have heartfelt skill?' And now look. I've got it."

Shauna directed me to park outside an old-time Berkeley coffeehouse, a place she'd once cruised for straight women go-ing through sexually experimental phases—preferring them, she told me, to real dykes, who either made Shauna feel too much the object of desire, voiding her own sexual agency, or else hu-mored her for a few weeks before declaring that what they really needed was pain, inflicted by Shauna. That period of her life stopped, Shauna told me, after a few unpleasant heartbreaks. "If I'm going to get screwed over by a big, selfish prick," Shauna said, leaning over our chamomile tea and ginger-molasses cookies on a wobbly café table, speaking up to be heard over the live Ashkenazi polka band, "I want it to be an actual prick, not just one that somebody sent away for." Parsing the scene around us, she pointed out two undergraduates, the cur-rent "baby dykes"—the more forceful of the two having bleached hair and a thick fur coat, a swagger in her gait. Shauna told me the woman's shaved eyebrows were the badge of the dominatrix, and that S&M was increasingly popular with the younger crowd—thus that satisfied look on her femme girl-friend's face. An appealing older woman waved hello with the self-confidence of the coolest guy in your high school, and Shauna waved back and blushed and leaned close to me, declar-ing this visit to this coffeehouse, with a man, a "major coming out for me."

Shauna's oldest friend showed up then, and while Shauna went to the women's room, her friend sat beside me, leaving her own boyfriend across the table. When Shauna returned, she made everyone move around so that she could sit next to me. Back home at last, she held me off even longer by dashing off an essay on how this bit of social etiquette was an unexamined legacy of eighteenth-century Restoration comedy, in which partner-swapping staved off the boredom of arranged political marriages. "I *always* want to sit next to you," Shauna wrote, "I want to feel my body temperature surge when I'm near you, when your shoulder brushes mine. We are not an old married couple who were rushed into an unhappy premature union and now have grown tired of each other's face . . . and people who still want to split up couples are just terrified by the threat that real intimacy poses to their fragile worlds. I mean, Hey, here are two people really *living*. What are the rest of us doing? Uh-oh . . . feel the walls come tumbling down."

Setting aside those just-printed pages, terrified as much as delighted, I helped Shauna onto her garlic-scented butcher block and pulled off her boots, her jeans—soft skin rubbing like life against the dead wood. "My fierce little fertility goddess," I said.

She stopped me. "I'm not sure I like the sound of that."

"No?"

"You ever seen one?"

"I don't know."

"They're generally quite plump. Which reminds me. Before we have sex. You're seeing somebody else, right?"

I swallowed.

"I'll consider that a yes." She exhaled, seemed to deflate slightly. She pushed me away from her and straightened her shirt. "And it's okay, Harper. You haven't promised me anything. And adults apparently date around, and we are apparently adults, and blah-blah-blah. Fine." She flopped onto her futon and leaned her head back and exhaled again. Then she said, "Do you know that I recently pulled a long blond hair out of this actor's chest hair—before I met you—and I was like, Hmm, what's this? He said, 'Oh, didn't you realize I was seeing other

people?' And I was like, 'No . . .' Anyway, he wanted his freedom, and I tried to tell him: Freedom's an ideological ruse!
We're never *really* free, anyway, are we? And hadn't he read the
Brothers K? Didn't he know the Grand Inquisitor saved us from
the anomie of freedom in the fifteenth century? I mean, it's just
another word for nothing left to lose! But he wasn't convinced.
He wanted to play the field. I was crushed."

I still couldn't speak.

"Harper, do you know that you flip out every time I even
imply a shared future? You really flip. You get mad at me."

I did not know this. But clearly, anything was possible.

"I mean, it's actually *not* psychotic for your lover—and
notice I didn't say girlfriend, so you wouldn't flip—but for her
to look forward. It's just not. And I think you're a great guy,
okay, I really do, with a gentle and innocent boy-spirit. I also
knew that would bother you, by the way, but you should see
your eyes when we make love—they're so sweet and yearning, and you shouldn't be embarrassed by that. I feel like you're
embarrassed by the way you are with me. Which I hate. I really
think I hate that. I'd want that to stop. Because I've spent a
lot of time alone, Harper, and I guess I'm sort of sick of it. I
guess I really want to move on to the next stage and be able
to be honest with somebody and not wonder what they're
doing when I'm out of town, or if they even like me at all.
Okay?"

"Of course."

"So maybe here's the deal: I don't want to see you again until you can be with me for real."

I nodded.

"Do we have a deal?"

I told her we had a deal.

"And I'm serious. No calls, no nothing."

"Deal."

"And I'll be waiting, okay. I'm not doing this because I don't have a crush on you. I'm going to be the girl waiting by the telephone, hoping every ring is you. But not if it's bullshit."

Thirty thousand feet over nighttime Montana, while the poor flight attendants passed out paper boxes holding cupcakes and potato chips, our evening meal, I settled into my exit-row seat and looked into the winter darkness and told myself that I could indeed keep a grip on my heart, I could indeed ask nothing of Joan. I was kidding myself, of course, but I tried to bear down on my heart the way you'd bear down with your jaw, and I told myself that an adult, independent man, of the kind I yearned to be, could accept the gift of Joan's time in Joan's city and even sleep in her very own bed and eat at her table and walk her streets and see the life she led away from me and not come undone. Sometime in the wee hours, the violent turbulence began, and I could feel the nervous exhaustion of the short and friendly stewardess carrying drinks and peanuts and the worry of some sorely missed home far below. All the eyes she saw, the sadness and deadness of travel, the transitions from one life to another—she seemed shaken and frightened by so much exposure, over so much time, to so many moving souls. With each lurch and dip I could also see that old whale's wings bowing and swaying in the winter blackness—the March freeze deep over the mountains. The whole cabin wiggled like a loose-jointed mechanical python, and a group of women in colorful body wraps began to chant in prayer for all of us, their voices lurching up an octave whenever the plane dropped, and I closed my eyes and said good-bye to everyone and everything, clutched the armrests, and felt more than heard the way those devout voices matched their earnest and saving argument to the very timbre and tone of the plane's roaring, dying one. A ferocious slamming noise turned out to be those same women banging Bibles against the walls of the plane, punctuating their insistence that our collective earthly errands remained undone by beating the love of God into that ancient plastic and steel rocket. Soon even the flight attendants deserted us, strapping themselves down to pray their perpetual, enduring, flight-attendant prayers, and for hour after hour the plane bounced and lurched and fell and caught itself, crashing over the snow-blanketed prairies, the frozen lakes, and snow-covered Appalachians.

To pass the time I read the newspaper: stock market soaring, tech industry minting sixty-four new millionaires a day. Jerry Yang, a computer scientist my age, had founded Yahoo! and was already worth $200 million. And there was this Craig McCaw guy, who just sold his cell phone company to AT&T for $1 billion, and Scott McNealy, worth $324 million from the meteoric success of Sun Microsystems. People were awfully rich, when you thought about it. But for what? For great ideas, that's what. I tried to think of a good idea. What did the world need? What technology had nobody thought of? I had no idea. But I shouldn't try to have an idea. That was the whole point now. On the back of the paper's front section I found an advertisement with a photograph of Charles Schwab, a nice-looking fellow with boyish parted hair and those wide eyeglasses that offend nobody. He had it all figured out, with your brokerage account here and your IRA there, and all these on-line tools for evaluating companies and even your own tolerance for risk. He made wealth seem so easy, Chuckie did—*a little common sense and you, too, will be loaded*. Apparently he had a book. "Go open yourself a Schwab account," my grandfather had once said. "And tell them your grandfather's a friend of old Chuck Schwab." What a crazy vision, heading down to the strip mall and telling the Schwab retail clerk, as he took my $200 starter check, "Hey, ah . . . by the way—if it makes any difference?—my grandfather's pretty tight with your founder here, so, ah . . . yeah, you know. Like that."

Dropping the newspaper, I pulled *Money* magazine from the seatback in front of me. Two handsome young assholes dominated the cover, smiling toothy grins aboard their yacht. A headline read, GET IT ALL, and THE ONDRICKS HAVE A FIRM GRIP ON THE SILVER EAGLE AND ON THEIR FINANCES. Smaller headlines said, *Retire Young the Smart Way, Double Your Money in Five Years or Less,* and *Secure Your Family's Future.* Inside, I saw an AT&T wireless ad with two intelligent-looking women my age in the backseat of a convertible, one smiling into a cell phone and the other just plain laughing out loud—happy corporate climbers with great clothes and great lives. Then I turned to a write-up on business schools, with an employment breakdown for Harvard MBAs showing 38 percent going into consulting at an average annual salary of $110,000, 14 percent in investment banking, at $85,000, high tech taking 11 percent, at $100,000, and private equity/LBO venture capital with 13 percent of Harvard MBAs earning $125,000. A course list for Columbia Business School, which made more sense, being in Manhattan: Finance, Human Resource Management, Managerial Accounting, Dynamics of Organizations, Strategy and Organization in the Global Economy. Life, apparently, was not about amusing yourself. It was about providing for those who depended on you. And maybe being European.

The plane landed before sunrise, and the JFK baggage claim

looked like American propaganda, with Puerto Rican families and Mexican bachelors and big Asian tour groups milling about the steel carousels, women in saris and Asian fraternity boys with headphones, and a handsome white man in a good houndstooth sport coat, slight of build and graceful of movement, with short sandy hair curling over a brow wrinkled in mahogany-paneled boardrooms and tanned on tropical golf courses. He carried a good briefcase and wore tortoiseshell glasses and bright yellow socks matching his bright yellow shirt. The belt, too—as if cut from the same cow as those beautiful light-brown loafers. His tan little daughter had a perfect camel-hair coat and a white bow in her sun-bleached hair, and she carried her own fashionable little luggage. Rich New Yorkers, I decided, looked a lot richer than other rich people. In the man's hands, I noticed a gift-wrapped box, and while I waited for my roller bag to appear, I thought, Dear God in heaven, will you please tell me why I'm so hardwired to want to become almost anybody else anywhere anytime? Like this complete stranger at carousel 5—who, like Gujie, is doubtless independent of heart, wallet, and sphincter, invulnerable of emotion and also long since over his mother, done with his father, and perfectly in touch with the calm strength at the center of his being. Why him? Why can't I just decide that I'm fine the way I am, and that it's wonderful that Shauna thinks the same, and get on with life?

"But maybe I wouldn't even care how much money you made," Joan had said, confusing matters as ever, in our last phone call before my flight. "Maybe you'd be the hunky guy giving me multiple orgasms in my bungalow."

"West Village," I told my cabdriver, and while I had no idea where that was, I enjoyed the words in my mouth. (What had Joan called it? A very obvious place to live?) The growing silver light brought out detail on every Honda Accord and every leaf-less winter tree, all the many material manifestations of the world in which Joan had for days been but a voice and a dream, the very seats of the cab sagging with the weight of substantial civilization. Wondering about the inbound rush of workers, their headlights on and their faces bent over their steering wheels, I began to see the bristling buttresses of the Manhattan skyline catching the cold violet light like sunrise in the high mountains. Then we soared over a fantastic black iron bridge and onto a chaotic avenue and down a steely canyon with steam rising from the sidewalks. He dropped me off where West Eleventh broke from the downtown grid at an eccentric angle, and I looked around at a narrow street of old-fashioned rust-red and brown townhouses with wrought-iron stair rails and bright brass doorknobs. Joan's address was in the middle of the block—a proper old apartment building painted white so long ago as to have weathered into an antique patina. I heard a child's voice from a basement-level window, and before I took those last steps across the threshold of Joan's building and into the vortex of her affection and rejection, I tried to steel myself by looking upward to the chilly morning sky bright blue with shining white clouds drifting in from the wintry forests of Pennsylvania, the cozy villages of New Jersey. The bare tree limbs branched out gray and spidery over a big-boned woman in a wool overcoat waiting patiently for her poodle to shit. The early-morning hum of Seventh Avenue came clear down the relative silence of West Eleventh, and a cold wind blew from the river as a tall young woman appeared in a doorway, her dark eyes sad and smart and brimming with insight. Oblivious to my stare, she skipped down the steps and off through the light dusting of snow, and I watched her go—imagined the books she read and the songs she liked, the places she wished she'd been and the old friends she was so glad she still had—figured she was probably loaded, too, from her family, but also determined to make her own life. Open to love, too, no doubt; eager for the right man to see the correspondence in their hearts and minds, and ask her to join him in celebration thereof. Looking again around her neighborhood, which was also Joan's neighborhood, I felt as if discovering the very center of a nurturing universe, of art and food and music and meaning. Joan lived here because Life was here, I thought, the World was here, tragedy and comedy, loss and nostalgia and plenitude and very pricey real estate. Turning on my heels, I looked around at a warren of human peace and sameness, of a good life arrived upon ages ago and maintained— the homes of fashionably dressed, well-read, and still-vital fathers consulting for ballet companies, museums, and universities (not separating money from meaning, retirement squared away), and bright-eyed mothers who sang their own literary jazz compositions on CDs with first-rate session men, and sons who went to Yale and became either ironic rock stars republishing long-neglected Eastern European poets on the side, on beautiful paper, or easygoing, quick-to-laugh concert pianists daylighting as neuroscientists.

But of course I had to keep those feelings to myself. I was a young man, lover to a young woman, come on a mission of sex and companionship and unattachment. I was a young man come for sex with a young woman in the world's greatest city. I was also in love, but those feelings had no place here, and I should be capable of accepting an erotic gift and not asking for more. I was not a sap with an aching heart. Suddenly giddy and scared on a cold March morning, I looked up at her building, a four-story brick affair with a marble-framed entrance. Shivering in the river wind, and knowing that I was getting in over my head, I looked across the street to a portly middle-aged man in a fur-collared black wool overcoat. His black hair swept back from a receding hairline, and behind tortoiseshell spectacles his eyes were captivated by me. He held a paper coffee cup in one leather-gloved hand, and as he sipped, he glared. Under the coat he appeared to be wearing a tuxedo. I turned as if to say hello, but then he walked away. In the foyer, I found 401 and stared at the intercom for a while. Then I hit the button and Joan's voice came crackling through, zooming with affection. Such proximity to the girl herself. I, down here; she, up above. Joan broke out laughing and buzzed me into the tired old lobby. The small elevator banged and clanged as the floors passed, lives and rooms and private joys, and when I stepped into a dark hallway, breathing deep to keep control, a black metal door cracked at the end. Bright white light flushed around Joan's silhouette.

"I can't believe it," she said softly.

"Hey, baby." My bag almost toppled on a carpet's edge as I rolled down the hall and stood at last before her. Joan's hair hung across the straps of a camisole, and the pale green silk lay against the brown of her breastbone, the smoothness of her arms. She smiled a half-bashful, half-stunned smile, and I found her so beautiful that I had to keep my mouth shut.

"You came all that way just to see me."

Indeed I had. And she certainly seemed happy about it. "Hey, how about letting me in?"

She laughed again and shook her head, undid the chain and blocked the door with her body. I leaned to kiss her.

She said, "Wait, tell me your name again?"

Be strong. "None of that. Just let me inside."

"No, please! Say something nice first. So I know for sure your intentions are good."

Okay, but be strong. "You're the most beautiful woman I've ever seen."

She opened the door and spread her arms, and I held my heart as tight as I could. Feel nothing, show nothing. She pulled me by the hand into a sun-flooded living area, French doors to a balcony and a dining alcove beside a tiled kitchen, bedroom to one side. Whoever had sublet this place to Joan—a working soprano, Joan told me—had very expensive tastes, and I think Joan felt embarrassed as she watched me take it all in—the dark leather sofa and chair, the glass and wicker coffee table, the sideboard full of china, and three black-and-white photographs of the fabulous Maria Callas singing Donizetti's *Lucia di Lammermoor.* A baby grand, half an acre of shining cherry wood, took up the living room, and a nearby bookshelf carried a collection of red hardbound Riccordi editions of Mozart's operas, the collected works of Verdi, Puccini. A built-in home entertainment center carried the large-screen TV and elaborate stereo of a person blighted by boredom; a burgundy kilim lay on the living room's blond wood floor. Two framed Chinese scrolls decorated one wall, alongside recently hung photographs of Joan herself, on stage, in college and high school. The white plaster curved around openings and bore framed bird prints, and glass doors opened to a sunny balcony. A low, cheap bookshelf carried the tattered remnants of what I assumed to be Joan's graduate school book collection, art theory and history and biography. The bed linens, at least, were Joan's, and as she slipped under her butterfly-print sheets, her very blankets and comforters reminded me of what I so loved: the feeling she always gave me that no place more than bed and no play more than the play of bed should occupy a lover's time and mind. I desperately wished we could just disrobe and make love and giggle and share everything and maybe stay in bed all day, but I was clearly unwelcome under the covers, so I rubbed my face in her hair.

"Sit up a second," Joan said. "Sit back away from me, okay? And don't touch me? I need to get used to this. I need to get my mind around it."

The sun shone outside, and Joan stared at me, eyes wide and a smile growing. She put a hand on each of my shoulders and squeezed. She ran her hands down my arms, held my wrists with her fingers, then held my palms, and I knew that disobeying her orders and touching back would be a mistake, a yielding of important ground. She stared at me, eyes wide, and then blinked and laughed and said, "Okay, okay. So let's get out of here. It's too intense. Let's go get breakfast or something."

Opening a closet to dress, Joan offering a glimpse of broadcloth shirts and silk blouses, sheer skirts and pressed slacks and strappy dresses on hangers, evening gowns and winter coats layered on hooks, and shoe boxes below and sweaters overflowing above. Baskets hung inside the door, spilling socks and lingerie. "Go out on the deck while I dress."

"Are you kidding?"

"Take your coat."

Passing through the living room, I looked again at the birdlike beauty of Maria Callas, and I wondered at the odd static quality of opera stills—people in funny costumes, standing around together. Then I did as told, finding that her apartment opened onto a cast-iron balcony. Across the way, a blond young man diligently prepared for his day, and I could see the office and apartment towers running to midtown. A fallow garden sat atop a four-story mansion, big boxes of dirt waiting for spring, and I noticed the same on Joan's balcony, empty planters and her mountain bike against a wall. I heard Joan's cell phone ringing inside, and I stayed out in the cold while she answered. She had a few lonely gardening tools on the deck, flower pots, a spilling bag of soil, and a box of snail poison. I sat on a cold iron bench and felt my cheeks chill, and I put my feet up on the iron rail and chose to savor the place, the possibility, everything that might or might not happen—the way you might feel on your first day of a hard-won new job you were no longer sure you wanted. When Joan had dressed, seeming glad to have me and annoyed with herself for being glad, we descended in the elevator—she in black pants and black zip-up boots, a charcoal-gray cashmere turtleneck, and a black leather car coat and sunglasses. We walked east on West Fourth, among the formal little townhouses, the narrow sidewalks with their green-wire trash baskets and blue *New York Times* vending machines. A small synagogue offered Music of the Jewish Mystics on Thursdays and bluegrass on Mondays. Good smells came from a body boutique, and a bundled-up mailman went about his work in sun shining bright. Clear and intelligent faces filled antique shops while an icy wind came off the river. Car alarms shrieked, diesel engines gurgled, and we walked over roaring subway grates and cellar hatch doors, through a neighborhood not of business or advertising but of urban human pleasures, the joys of African art and leather handbags, used guitars and fresh fish. The great visual world of Manhattan was the perfect foil for Joan's naturally dramatic sense of self, and I crushed the impulse to put an arm around her, to hold her tight. Looking elsewhere, I stared into anonymous pedestrian eyes, heard the clanging and rushing din, and smelled garbage and exhaust and coffee, scones and ammonia.

"You feel . . ." Joan said. " . . . What is it?" She took her cell phone from her pocket, glanced at its screen. "You feel solid. Why?"

I had no idea.

She glanced again at her phone. "It's quite appealing."

Hoping to leaven the mood, in a burlesque of Joan's training, I walked on the curb side of the sidewalk and dodged a lamppost and then a garbage can, protecting Joan from the imaginary dangers of the street. She laughed and told me to cut it out and act naturally. So I did, enjoying the grinding visual variety of old and new, of people drinking and eating and talking. The press of taxis and buses, the sheer movement of the old and the young, the free and the burdened—at Bleecker and Sixth Avenue, while a slack-haired little girl held her mother's hand in cold air smelling of bacon and intermittently warm with the fleeting updrafts of dank subway stations, we stood a moment outside a building in which a well-known audition coach had a studio—"You sing a few bars of a standard," Joan said, "and then he leaves the room and comes back with the exact, perfect audition number for your voice." Joan rubbed my arm with her shoulder, and so I put my arm around her, but she wriggled free and left me chasing through the clanging and rushing din, whispering, *Fuck, I love you*. Still slightly ahead, Joan spoke on her cell to someone I assumed to be Agnes—there was mention of the evening plan and a lot of "No, no, no, you terrible girl" from Joan. Through crowd after crowd of specific, dreaming humans, she led me, subways roaring below, taxi armadas swerving and swarming. A car radio played Queen's "We Are the Champions" while church bells tolled and the smells of stale beer and bagels and newsprint mingled on McDougal Street. Joan seemed to be walking just to walk, as though deciding what we were doing together before she allowed us to arrive. Pigeon shadows flitted across the asphalt, and we passed a dilatory father-son street hockey game, a couple eating eggs at a window table. A toothless old woman, remnant of some vanished New York, wept outside an apartment building she apparently could not reenter. Across roaring Houston, among the big brick-and-steel SoHo loft buildings, the sexy youths and tourists and older couples disposing of income, I felt everywhere, as if for the very first time, the sheer joy people took in looking fantastic; I heard the loud click of great new boots expressing a thousand great possible selves, and delivery trucks beeping their backing-up beeps and workmen hurling scrap lumber from high windows, the boards banging into big Dumpsters. New to the sheer volume of it all, I looked in every face, every set of eyes, worried for some and smiled with others, yearned to live lives conjured and to be that passing man and to trade Valentines with that warm-eyed, competent woman waiting for a cab. A little boy whispered to his street-vendor father, and a double-decker tour bus paused roaring in the street, some inane voice bellowing on a bullhorn.

Outside a reproduction of a Parisian brasserie, hand-painted window signs advertised *café express, petit déjeuner*, and *croque monsieur*. Opening the door, Joan followed a thirtyish couple-with-baby into a dining room of steamed milk and butter smells, ham and chocolate and salmon, lights embedded in the columns and varnished dark wood partitions and a hammered-tin ceiling, zinc bars and big mirrors. She glanced again at her cell phone, and again didn't answer it. The cheerful bob-haired hostess seated the young parents first, and then us beside them, at a red leather banquette with a window view, the river of humans hustling past outside. We sat in what for me was a familiar loaded silence while Joan stared at the skinny new mom, who was dressed all in black with government-issue clunky artist shoes and her brown hair in a bun—perhaps a sculptress caught in the exhausted, exhilarated countdown to her first solo show. I kept expecting Joan to start talking, to tell me something, but she didn't, and I distracted myself by looking at the young father, with prematurely gray hair and clothes studiously hip in a kind of 1950s auto mechanic–fly fisherman idiom. He was having an out-of-body love-of-baby-girl moment, and I wouldn't have minded being him. Not one bit.

Commuters hustled past, and some lined up for coffee at the café counter and then vanished again. Joan looked around the room, radiating impenetrability. "I can see," she said at last, with compassion, as if she knew how weird she could be, "that you don't know what to do with yourself."

I shook my head: correct.

"You're being very brave."

I smiled.

"Ask me what I want to eat and drink."

So I did, and then laughed when she thanked me and said she'd just love a double cappuccino and something called a *pain bagnat.* I raised my hand for a waiter.

"Don't be rude," Joan said. "Just go up and ask him quietly."

I did, and he was very pleasant, and I ordered myself a *jambon Gruyère* and stepped outside to buy a *New York Times.* A waiter set down our coffee and Joan took the front section. While she read, I watched the sidewalk grow less busy, the pre-work rush having passed.

It was early afternoon by the time we finished breakfast, and Joan declared a desire to go shopping. She led me first into a small boutique filled with confusing frills of brassieres and camisoles and bustiers and garters, teddies and thongs. The place had an air of self-respect, its wood floors gleaming, the walls painted a clean, new cream. The coiffed little cashier sat in a garden of pinks and greens and purples and blacks, of skin-cream colors and virginal whites and bright reds. She smiled at Joan as if they recognized one another, as if this tiny shop held the real source of private pleasure in the life of a truly discerning woman. Glancing around, I was overcome by the unpleasant realization that I had never seen a single item of lingerie—beyond the odd camisole—on a flesh-and-blood woman. The image, in fact, had always left me confused: what could be sexier than skin itself? Well, something, certainly, or we wouldn't be here, and while Joan ignored me and browsed and I wondered at the values and choices implied by lingerie, and whether they meant I really *had* wasted my life thus far, I sat on a plush love seat and looked through soft-porn lingerie catalogues and occasionally watched Joan scan a rack of peignoirs, or satin robes, or sheer hose, as if this were a serious hobby or a favorite pastime. After half an hour in a dressing room, she asked for my credit card to buy a silk bustier—she'd forgotten her wallet—and then we were back in the pedestrian push and Joan's face worked its way around some thought.

I asked, "Yeah? What is it?"

"Mmm . . ."

"Come on, talk to me."

"Nah, I changed my mind. But tell me something, how many lovers have you had?"

"What?"

"Just tell me."

"Why?"

"My God, it must be millions."

"It's not millions. It's just a dumb topic."

"You're the one who apparently wants full disclosure."

"How many lovers have you had?"

"I asked you first."

"What if my number's too small?"

"You're right," she said. "I do want it to be hundreds. I want you to have had countless lovers."

"It's probably between twenty-five and thirty."

"Me, too," Joan said quickly. "But don't get all excited about something we've got in common. That's not what we're doing here." A men's store window display caught Joan's eye. "And hey, this," she declared, pulling me inside, "is *exactly* what you need." She held up a sport coat: silver, faux-fur, fish-scale pattern, a thousand dollars on sale. "Just put it on," she said.

So I did.

"You're so handsome."

Scooting for a mirror, I asked if she really thought it was flattering.

"You're so handsome." Turning to a beautiful Puerto Rican salesman, six-three and outrageously thin and muscular and smooth-skinned, Joan said, "Doesn't he look like a rock star?"

The salesman laughed a grand, toothy laugh, and I blushed at him, and he nodded with weary approval. "You do wear that well," he said. He was a magnificent specimen, in tailored charcoal slacks and a tight black turtleneck.

Joan said, "Cash, I'm serious. Is it your size?"

I looked to the salesman again, and his face acquired an affectionate professionalism, zeroing in on my shoulders, my waist.

"But you know, baby," I said to Joan, "I don't have the money for . . . "

"You understand nothing about life. Is that his size or not?"

The salesman stood close and square in front of me, tugging here and there. He said, "Mmm . . . might have to be let out a little. You lift weights, don't you?"

I blushed, shook my head.

"He's a surfer," Joan said. "He lives in California."

The salesman nodded. "It's all that volume in the front of your chest."

I loved this guy.

"Wow, you are the biggest flirt," Joan said, as I walked out the door as fast as I could, "and you really don't want the coat?"

We stopped next at ABC Carpet & Home, Joan marching across the plank-floored showroom and swinging with the live jazz quartet and the well-heeled customers among ornate Indonesian cabinets, Second Empire ottomans, and Chinese chairs. She trailed a fingertip along a $4,000 British colonial table and skipped through the huge parlor floor with its hand-blown Venetian chandeliers hanging over faded mosaic tables, jewel-toned crystal glasses, and antique French copper cookware. How even do the math to calculate the yearly incomes of the consumers of such things? Especially with a wallet like mine? And there, again, went Joan's departing hips, and so I followed, dancing from dining set to dining set, and as I followed, I began to lose myself in their movement, the way they bespoke a lifetime as a thing wanted by better men than I, spent not like my own life, saying, "Can I? Can I? Can I? Can I? Really?" but rather, "No, no, no, no, no, well . . . maybe." Such certainty this woman had! Such a capacity to believe in herself in this moment in this place! For all her faults and all her madness, all her infuriating and persistent distance from me, she did know how to affect a truly compelling persona, and I wished very much that I could do the same. But perhaps it wasn't such an easy trick, perhaps it was a function of walking in a world defined by its universal desire for you and availability to you, of strolling the world's great bazaars with the delicious implication that every Peruvian rose farmer delivering to the Cuzco airport, every broken-down Kashmiri shepherd and big-sky ranch hand and sclerotic truck driver balling the jack past midnight, even the air traffic controllers of the great gridlocked airports and the very bomber pilots keeping the world safe for capitalism, the small Latin American rebel movements fighting and falling and rising again and the cassock warriors struggling with the Windows Operating System—everyone was doing it for Joan Artois herself, as if she were the one precise woman for whom this grand world worked.

In a room of beds nicer than I'd ever imagined, the beds of kings and queens, Joan lay on a wooden four-poster selling for $3,200—in the amber glow of some ancient chandelier for the low, low price of $1,450—and she whispered my name. I had never even seen furniture this expensive, except perhaps without knowing it in the Cavanaugh home. With my eyes on an especially fine set of mustard-colored sheets, I heard Joan whisper again. I turned to look, saw her face resting on a hydrangea-strewn $400 pillow and her charcoal-colored wool skirt pulled up just enough to reveal that she wasn't wearing any underwear above those garter-belted black stockings. She pulled the skirt higher to show the soft patch of auburn hair. "Oh dear God," I said, "don't we ever get to go home together?" Joan laughed with delight and said, "But how do I know I can trust you?" She stood up and pressed her mouth to mine. "My goodness," she said, "at least I'm lucky to be wanted this much." But then she was gone again, and I followed her past love seats and children's beds to an eight-motherfucking-thousand-dollar mahogany-framed daybed covered with spreads of lovely fabrics I'd never even seen before and piled with velvet and silk pillows, all of it bound for the homes and rooms of lives I'd never even heard of, the lives of exquisitely educated, well-mannered millionaires with genuinely rich and varied sex lives. "Come on," I whispered over her shoulder, "just for a few hours. I won't even take for myself. I will bury my face and only give." A sign forbade sitting on the beds, and Joan said, "Look at this stuff. You see, as nice as cunnilingus can be? The truth is that I love bed linens above all." She drew her skirt upward again and fell directly upon the daybed, looked around the room, and said, "Really, Cash, I mean, what's the big deal?"

"Are you out of your mind?" I asked, worried about being caught, but even more worried about being caught by Joan in the act of being worried. "I'm going to die," I told her. "Right here, if you won't let me take you home."

"Aren't you hungry, anyway?"

"Only for you."

"But what if I want you to buy me dinner first?"

Not just beds, actually, but entire bed *regimes*. Not just the usual sheets and comforters, but neck rolls and all manner of duvets and deep cushions and varieties and patterns I lacked the tools even to describe, much less appreciate.

"But why does this particular sight do that to you?" Joan asked. "The sight of *mine*. I really don't get it."

"What's not to get?" Dust ruffles! Bed skirts! Flower prints and stripes and paisleys and silks and . . .

"I mean, I know men like to see that, but why do *you*?"

"I am a man of hunger, okay? I *want*. That's all I am. Wanting. Everything. You. Sex. Money. Power."

Kneeling beside her, I reached between her legs and picked up the edge of the deep purple silk sheet—unbelievably smooth.

"But what could possibly be attractive to you about my actual pussy?" Joan asked. "There's nothing beautiful about it."

The hell with country cotton, I decided. "Your pussy doesn't have to be beautiful. You could make a fortune just letting people photograph it. Beauty only attaches to secondary traits, to feet and noses and breasts, not to genitals themselves."

"It still doesn't make sense." Joan dropped her skirt, and I moved toward her until she stood up and marched off again. "If I'm taking you anywhere at all, you have to tell me more. Help me understand."

Trotting behind, I said, "I'm genetically hardwired to lose my mind with desire at the sight and smell of your pussy. That's it. A million years of evolution. End of story." Oh, and also, I love you I love you I love you I love you.

"But why?" Somehow, Joan *was* every bed in that place. And I? A pretender to the throne of this queen's king, a phony wanting to drag this woman into the fire escape. Burgundy silk "throws," five hundred dollars. Salespeople everywhere. Men in shockingly beautiful clothing. I'm from California! I don't know about people like this. Fragrances! Chandeliers! Oh, the boudoir! "There doesn't have to *be* a why to it," I called after Joan as she marched laughing and beckoning from Ralph Lauren into Classics, through Palais Royale and toward the freight elevator. "There doesn't even have to be an aesthetic explanation! Your pussy's beauty-as-beauty precedes aesthetics. It is the very Platonic form of the desired object."

Joan said it was time for steak and wine, so we ate at a polished-wood bar with men in suits laughing, and Joan chatted with two of them. I thought, *And hey, maybe this is what she wants, anyway, an up-and-coming businessman type, late thirties, good teeth.* And I was an academic, and there was nothing wrong with that. I wasn't the kind of guy to blow discretionary income on clothes of a more edgy stripe than his boring (but sensibly lucrative and stable) career would normally indicate, and on food and drink and fancy crap for his apartment. The kind to go shopping with a work buddy on a Thursday afternoon. And the truly extraordinary women of the world, the Clare Boothe Luces and Francines and Joanie Artoises, would always draw attention like this and would always feel entitled to enjoy it. As her indestructible lover, of the kind I would have to become, I would wish she'd stop flirting, sure, but mostly I'd worry about her embarrassing herself; I'd be such an immovable force that she couldn't hurt me if she tried. Because I'd care only about the fact that I was the one she truly loved. I was the one she needed, the one to whom she always returned. Although one of these assholes, I could see, was already beaming with the self-confidence Joan elicited so effortlessly from me, too. What was it, anyway? The way she looked at you so steadily while you spoke? Nodding her head, her deep brown eyes alternately widening with amazement and sinking with inner awe? I could even hear her asking smart, insightful questions about exactly how fascinating this prick really was, her gaze dwelling on his mouth as he responded. And now he was getting the predictable and acute sensation that this lovely woman was thinking deeply sexual thoughts about him, that she was somehow intuiting the essence of his unknown erotic self. Yep, there he went: his flattered vanity mistaking her spell for his own prowess, and now he was pushing it. Pretty soon, of course, if I knew my girl, she'd withdraw just a little, let some crack linger a little too long in the air, so that it came to seem inadequate and even wrongheaded, as if this beauty had pitched him a slow ball and he'd fouled it afield. Like a winning gambler losing his first hand and betting more on the next childhood anecdote, the next promise of great success in his immediate future, it wouldn't work somehow, and in no time at all he'd feel boastful and foolish and worthy only of contempt.

And what was that guy doing, anyway, looking at his watch to tell Joan the time? Nice watch, actually. A big dive watch of some kind, which was a little silly for a guy dining in Manhattan. A guy who wouldn't have known what to do with a surfboard in one-foot Waikiki, much less eight-foot Ocean Beach. But wow, what a hunk of metal. But then they were leaving, anyway, and as I paid our own check, I glanced at my black plastic digital, a cheap Timex Ironman copied right off my father's wrist, making an ascetic declaration that I recused myself from the economies of status and desire that drove people to buy fancy watches. While Joan drained the last of her drink, I muttered something about buying a watch with moving hands and a leather band. Joan was always up for such an errand, and she led me down a glittering block of lower Broadway, in and out of various watch and jewelry boutiques. I tried on a Spanish-styled Festina Titanium Cobra and a heavy metallic Chase-Durer Blackhawk MACH 3 Alarm Chronograph, even a Men's U.S. Special Forces Underwater Demolition Team Chronograph Watch. Fabulous hunks of highly endowed steel, and yet they made me increasingly unhappy, sweaty and itchy, so I tried on a sleek little Calvin Klein Bold Square Citizen and a Promaster Cyber Aqualand NX, but they were much too fashionable and much too expensive, and looking at them reminded me of how bad I sucked and also how much of an ass I was for thinking this meant that I sucked. Had I not always harbored a special disdain for men who wore big diving-style watches, trafficking with inauthentic identities, advertising their compensation issues? And yet, and yet, was I not also beginning belatedly to understand that clothing was nothing but sexual display and that the very notion of an authentic self-in-clothes was only a necessary illusion of the frantic young? In that context, my own digital watch was no more than a badge of allegiance to a fictitious identity—to that of a man with good values. And what about this embarrassing wallet of mine, sitting on the copper watch-store countertop? Forest green woven nylon with Velcro closures? Perhaps likewise a contributing factor in the gaping sense of emptiness at the center of my being? I'd had that wallet since college, when I'd bought it for $4.99.

"I'm getting confused," Joan said, as we left yet another store. "What exactly are you looking for, in a watch?"

I couldn't say. Couldn't even say aloud the fact that I couldn't say.

"I mean, is it price? Do we need to find something cheaper?"

My whole face locked into a mask as I nodded. Yeah. Something cheaper.

At a drugstore, Joan browsed lipstick while I bought a thirty-dollar Timex Outdoor Casual Metal Tech watch and felt a wave of happiness (except for a twinge of shame over that annoyingly lame wallet) because I knew that thirty dollars was exactly my price point for a watch, and that I had somehow found the courage to stick to my guns, to be the man I truly was. Then we walked outside and I realized that I had bought a piece of shit that would break down in a few months, and that Joan probably thought less of me already.

Stopping at yet another bar, Joan suggested I order a round of cosmopolitans. Paying the waitress, I pulled out my green nylon Velcro wallet and handed over a credit card and then accepted the realization that had been dawning on me for over an hour, that the wallet, not the watch, was the real reason for the gaping sense of emptiness at the center of my being. It was an embarrassment, not at all the kind of wallet that held the kinds of credit cards that bought fabulously expensive bustiers for women like Joan and then fell to the floor in the Versace suit pants of men who got to fuck women like Joan while those women were wearing said bustiers. Looking at the other men in the bar—real men, adult men—I wondered at the wallets they carried. Clearly, they had not considered waterproofness or lightness of weight in their purchases of wallets. They had known, from the beginning—as if born with the knowledge— that wallets are accessories, worn in pants in cities and produced at sensitive moments. Wallets are, in essence, the packaging for a man's economic power and proof of identity. So how could I have so long imagined wallets meaningless? Or had my cheap sports wallet not actually *been* a declaration of meaning? Well, of course it had been, like the watch. Practicality, functionality, cheapness (thrift, then, as a subset of practicality, in the assembling of a personality)—these had been my considerations. I was the kind of guy who owned digital sports watches and Velcro sports wallets and therefore wasted no money on frivolities, on worldly distractions. The kind of guy, in short, who imagined that he kept his eyes fixed firmly on higher values, higher things. Clearly a misbegotten, childish theory of identity. Never challenged, and so never changed. Based on fear, weakness: if I acknowledge the free-floating nature of identity, the fact that a watch that looks like a dive watch is merely a simulacra like all the others around me, that I've never run an Ironman triathlon nor intend to, then where are the firm anchors? Well, it doesn't matter anymore, does it? Because I'm going to grow out of this, accept identity as malleable, and embrace the power of accessories.

When I'd paid for a final cab ride, Joan let me follow her

into her apartment, refusing to explain what on earth was happening. "Ah . . . the surfer boy," she said, dropping her coat and undressing. "So curious!" She hopped under her comforter and stared at me. While I undressed, she said, "I'm still not completely sure how we're going to do this."

"You're not?"

"I need something to work with."

"Like what?"

"Like your fantasy. Your ultimate fantasy."

"You really want to hear it?"

She laughed, apparently guessing what I meant, and then she pulled me beside her. She said, "Okay, okay. Let me decide."

"Decide what?"

"What we're doing together, silly." She rested her chin on my chest, thinking. "All right, how's this: what if I'm a prostitute?"

"What?"

"Not a streetwalker. Just a nice call girl."

But why?

"And my name is Dawn."

Naturally.

"And . . . maybe you're just in town as a tourist. But it's not like I have a bad life. I've got my own place and I teach some aerobics and I get to buy jewelry, which I totally love. And maybe I just met this cute California surfer named Cash and he seemed so sweet that I was happy to fuck him for free."

I wondered if it would be better to be a john. At least johns had money.

"Should I *try* being a whore?"

"Are you serious?"

"I do need a new career. And I should've been getting paid for what I've done for you."

I chuckled, nervous.

"How much do you think I'd get?"

"From me?" Very little. Because I had so little.

"In general, if I was a whore?"

"I don't know." I hated this conversation. I didn't want her to be a whore.

"Guess, though. How much would men pay to sleep with me?"

I'd personally pay whatever it would take to keep her from sleeping with anyone else. "I don't know how much guys would pay, baby. For one go? A thousand dollars, maybe?" She appeared insulted, so I said, "Well, shit. What do I know? Maybe it's more like ten grand. Or twenty. I bet it's twenty."

"See, I could enjoy that."

This was becoming painful. I wanted Joan not to be a whore. I wanted her not even to want to be a whore, or even to think it was fun to talk about. I wanted her to stop this.

"Would you ever go to one?" Joan asked.

"I don't think so, Joan."

"What if I paid for it?" She smiled.

"Joan, I just don't know if that's for me."

"Not even for a blow job?" She laughed, reaching for a *Village Voice*. "Come on! I'll find an ad and pay for it, and even hold your hand, if it'll make you happier."

Now I was thoroughly miserable. I couldn't speak at all.

"This isn't working for you, is it? It's not working for you. Okay." So she grabbed a copy of *Vogue* and straddled me and laid the magazine on my chest. "Okay," she said, "then lighten up, humor me for a while, take my mind off my troubles. Tell me who's hotter. Here: Naomi or Kate." She flipped the page over for me to see.

I laid a palm on each of her bare coppery hips and said, "Mm . . . Naomi."

"How about Elle?"

The six-foot paragon of hourglassed female physical perfection wore a silk Burberry scarf aboard a yacht in Monte Carlo.

I said, "You," and I meant it. I wasn't being nice. My hands swept up the curve to her waist and ribs, imprinting their memory. "Elle has nothing on you," I said. "I mean that."

"Have you ever met anyone who needed so many compliments?"

I had not, but the truth was, I liked Joan for this, and I liked being the guy who gave those compliments. "Here's the deal," I told her. "Elle's got a perfect figure and a pretty face, but she exudes no carnal knowledge. She looks like a big innocent." I skimmed Joan's stomach with the back of my hand. "You're gorgeous, but it's your weird intelligence that makes you the sexiest woman of all time. It's your freakish understanding of desire."

"Cassius, do you really think I'm that sexy? You're such a sweetheart."

"Take your ass, for example. Do you know you have a miraculous ass?"

She twisted back to look. "I do, don't I?"

"It's the Platonic form of Good Female Ass. But you know this?"

"I know that men always say that."

"Well, my very capacity to want, Joan, is leaving behind the world of women and settling on your ass. The rest of you, of course, too. It's like the dimensions of your hips or something, right here, and these two shoulders . . . and the ratio of your forehead to your chin, it's all resolving into the very type of beauty for me—colonizing my ideal and becoming not a woman I'm seeing but the only woman in the world." Why was I doing this? Why was I performing devotion under this absolutely firm agreement that we not even consider a future together?

"Do you do this for all the other women in your life?"

"There are no other women."

"That's a lie."

"Even before I met you, there were no other women. It's always been you."

"Tell me which breasts you like better." Joan was at the magazine again. "Hers, or hers?"

"Yours."

"What do you really think of my breasts, though? I mean, I'm basically flat-chested."

"Okay, you want the scoop? For men? Volume's not so important. It's mostly about sphere and nipple placement, and see, look." I pushed *Vogue* aside and presented Joanie exhibits A and B. "Even the distribution of volume, in the ideal breast, would follow your model. Because, you know, upon inspection? Upon a caress? Hold still. Let me sit up. See, you actually have world-class tits."

"But they stopped growing."

"Isn't that natural, though?"

"Early, I mean. Because my mother never loved me."

"You don't honestly believe that."

"She stunted my growth."

"Does your mother have large breasts?"

"No, but her mother was mean as hell, too. I just want big ones. I want hooters."

"But yours are perfect already."

"Except for volume."

"Not true. There's the requisite handful. But the bigger issue is really the nipples: size, shape, placement, orientation relative to the breast's hemispheres and zeniths. Small, hard, and upright, in your case, and pointing up and to the side like this raspberry right here. And see, stop giggling."

"Oh . . . I got a bad feeling."

Her laughter filled me with the hope I'd been trying to suppress, and I asked, "A bad feeling about what?"

"I think Cupid's in the room somewhere."

Did she say Cupid?

She said Cupid.

Last time I checked, Cupid was all about love.

And how could she bring up Cupid if she didn't love me? Right now? How could she intend that to mean anything but that she was starting to love me?

"Oh, why *is* it," she asked, giggling again, "no really, *why?* It's so unfair! All you have to do—tsk, it's so pathetic—all you have to do is suck on that one nipple like this and here I go, here I go, no resistance to the pushy Mr. Harper. It's like you hit a light switch or something, and all of a sudden, no matter what deep thoughts Dawn was going to think today or what she wants to be when she grows up, you get to have her. But, baby, indulge me one last time before you do me. It's so lame, but I'm like this, I just am. Please, please, remind me of why you like me so much."

Like you? I thought. "Because you're the single loveliest woman of all time."

"You really think that?"

"Absolutely hands down. You have no idea."

She named a string of movie actresses, testing yet again the firmness of my belief. I passed handily.

"I'm going to be forty in ten years," Joan said. "Will I still be sexy then?"

"Only more so. Because you'll know even more about desire than you do now, and your gorgeousness will have deepened. And your true sexiness is in your attitude, anyway; it's that freakish knowledge you have of how the human heart works."

She giggled, growing happier. "Why am I so obsessed with aging? Eliza's actually excited about it. She thinks she'll be so wise and wonderful. But okay, how about when I'm fifty?"

Perhaps I'd even know her then! "Sexier still."

"Sixty?"

Sure! "It's in the bones, Joanie, the facial architecture, and you've got it in spades. Some women's beauty falls with their skin. Yours won't." (Where did I get this crap? From my crazy mother, distinguishing between two old girlfriends of mine. And how sick is that?)

"God, you're good at that! And okay, come on. This is all getting a little too personal. If you really don't want Dawn the hooker, you've got to tell me what you *do* want."

I just stared at her. Because what I wanted was *her*. I wanted Harper to make love with Joan.

"Right, right," she said, dashing into her closet again. "I forgot." A moment later she emerged in penny loafers with a white blouse and plaid skirt—a burlesque of a Catholic school-girl's outfit. I laughed out loud. "What are you doing?"

"Come on," she said. "Help me out here. Play."

"Play?"

"What do you want me to do?"

I hadn't a clue.

"Seriously, Opie. I'm in your office, after school."

"My office."

"Sure, and . . . maybe you're my soccer coach. I don't know. Make this work. You told me I'd better come see you after school, because of how I've been behaving at practice."

"Okay, go put your hands on that table over there." I pointed to her bed. "Because I really am pretty sick of you." And I was. So I pulled up this little plaid skirt and found, be-neath the uniform of the Convent of the Sacred Heart, lime-green satin garters holding up those regulation white hose, and no underwear at all. "You terrible girl," I said. "Is this what you came to my office for?"

But what the hell else did one say? And were these really the final archetypes? This Central Casting lineup of good men brought low? But I told her I'd been watching her in practice for weeks, and that I'd gotten tired of her little games, and we were going to have to do this every day after school for the rest of the term. That I might even have to spank this young ass, just like that, and like that, and show her in no uncertain terms that she behaved the way she did and dressed the way she did precisely so that this would happen, and now it was happening, and there was no getting out of it until I was good and done with her. In fact, she might have to learn to turn around just now and kneel on the floor and . . .

She stepped into her changing room yet again, and while I sat awkwardly on the bed, I watched Joan's shadow flicker in the closet's off-cast light. I heard the clink of ice in her glass. Joan danced back into sight with a "Ta-da!" wearing her old Hamlin basketball uniform.

"What is this?"

"You don't want to be another coach?"

I didn't want to be anything at all.

"You don't. I can see it in your eyes." She pointed a pistol finger at me, pulled the trigger, and said, "Back in a flash." More thrashing in the closet, and I kicked off my shoes and stood up to remove my jacket, and then Joan stepped into the room again with her hands on the hips of tan cashmere slacks topped by a matching jacket and white blouse.

"Ah . . ."

"Oh . . . bleagh." She hopped again out of sight as I rubbed my face and wondered what was going on.

Joan peeked around the closet door. "Ready?" She wore only a silk bodice now—aged nineteen, she told me, bashful at the sheer presence of her new woman's body and meeting a nice boy on a train, wearing for him her first piece of sexy clothing. Joan's costume filled the space before my frustrated eyes, and I let Joan hold my hand to her mouth and kiss my fingers, and I tried to see clearly the bodice's handiwork, an ancient human art forgotten only in my childlike outpost of a frontier culture. Where had I been all these centuries, I wondered, as Joan drew that hand of mine between her legs, set my fingertips on the small snap buttons. "See?" she asked. "See how it works?" The snaps popped and the tautness of the cloth loosened over Joan's open brown navel and I felt a welling confusion. Such a civilized power, that outfit bespoke, flattering and presenting the timeless miracle. Looking from stitch to stitch to the muscle line of Joan's infuriatingly smooth shoulder, her sinewy singer's neck, I looked also around the room, at a framed piece of Bernstein sheet music and an exuberant promotional poster from *Guys and Dolls*. The chamber itself was such a lucky space—a bookshelf held Joan's old paperbacks of Cervantes and Borges, Lorca, Neruda, and García Márquez, Goethe's *Sorrows of Young Werther* and a New Grove Beethoven biography—and I felt like a mistreated tourist on a guided Sunday walk-through, wishing I could see *la vrai France*. The closet door hung open, the light was still on, and I saw a lingerie treasure trove overflowing from a wire basket, fit for Restoration drama or the secret life of a corporate vixen. And bought when? For and by whom? Just by Joan, in a lifelong indulgence? Worn alone on that luscious couch with a solo martini and a Verdi CD? Or, as was far more likely, carrying the peculiar specificity and unshakeable memory of other boys like me. "My goodness," Joan was saying, all arch amusement, "my boy-from-train, you really *are* the quintessential virile young man, aren't you? And *wow*, okay, because whatever boy-from-train says, there is no way that was love. Nor *that*. God, boy is brutal. I *knew* it. I could tell. Heavens, somebody must have hurt boy's feelings! No, no, *no*, don't slow down because I said that! Don't be such a momma's boy! It's *okay* to be mad in life! You're a fucking angry guy, and you should be! It's written all over your face." Rolling away, she said, "Jeeza-loweeza, Opie, you can put me on my back and make me come. It's a whole new missionary."

I nodded.

"Okay, what else should I wear?"

"I don't care."

"Come on, really. What should I wear? What's your fantasy?"

"You don't want to know my fantasy."

"Oh, but I do. And you're a genuine pervert, by the way."

"Is that true?"

"You were holding out on me all that time." She pulled a floor-length mink over nothing at all, and then she asked, "What are you doing?"

"Putting on jeans."

"Why?"

"Hell, I don't know. To be wearing clothes, like you."

This was intensely upsetting to her: "Off."

Sitting nude and denatured and more or less alone, I met a precocious girl in a one-piece Speedo swimsuit and plastic flip-flops, fresh from an hour of practicing her double gainers on the country club high dive—following the buff lifeguard into the pool house.

Joan lit a cigarette, sat on the floor.

I asked, "How exactly am I a pervert?"

" 'Suck it hard, bitch, like you want to swallow me whole'?" Then, miraculously, a woman prisoner, the only thing that really came to mind for me with Joan: the one who'd been fistfighting too much in the yard. Here she was asking if once again I might exact my own private punishment instead of sending her to that horrible warden. But it all felt as if running away from me again—Joan and my heart and whatever I'd thought I was doing here. And I found myself trying one more time to give that elusive one hundred percent, a level of violence I couldn't believe Joan wanted, until my whole lifetime's objectless hatred was getting shaped and channeled right through her and she was saying, "Wow, you are finally learning how to fuck me. It's so wonderful."

I said, "I'm not sure I've ever had sex before."

"What do you mean?"

"I'm just not sure I've ever known the first thing about sex."

"And you *still* won't tell me your ultimate fantasy?"

"You mean my *ultimate* fantasy?"

"Think I can handle it?"

"You really want to know my ultimate fantasy?"

"What, is it really creepy or something?"

I took a long, slow breath, and I saw a flicker of fear in Joan's eyes.

She laughed. "It was just a playful question."

But she'd given me a sign, I'd read that sign, and I simply could not control myself any longer. I didn't want to control myself any longer. I was done playing games. I said, "See, Joan, here's the problem. The problem is that my ultimate fantasy— the real, depth-of-my-heart, private-night-thoughts fantasy—the one that gets me rock-hard at night when I'm alone is this: it's thinking of you loving me."

She pushed back to stare.

"And that's it. That's my whole fantasy."

"Cash, what are you doing?"

"What do you mean?"

"We're having so much fun."

"What's . . . I know. That's why I'm telling you I'm in love with you. I'm completely in love with you."

"Oh God, Cassius."

"And it's been killing me. It's been horrible. I kept thinking I could be all strong and cool and detached, and I was wrong."

"But you barely know me. What if you get to know me better and you find out you don't like me?"

"Impossible."

"It's not impossible at all. And why do you think I'm so special, anyway?"

"You're dynamite, Joan. A little vulgar, a little volatile, but dynamite. And you're about as sexy as they come."

"Okay, see, but that's the problem. That's what you're really saying. You're not saying you love me. You're saying you like fucking me."

"Joan, don't do this."

"What do you think you love, though?"

"I love your vulnerability, I love the meandering course of your life. I love your weird brain."

"See, that's just the crap everybody always tells me."

"And that's the knockout who doesn't believe in herself."

"But I'm not even a knockout, Harper. And that's why I think this might be all in your head."

"But I'm not saying you're gorgeous, anyway, because you're not. You're a pretty woman, but you're not nearly as pretty as your presence. It's all in the force of your personality."

This appeared to relax her slightly. She said, "But I still don't believe you're in love with me. I think you're in love with some idea you have."

"Is that right?"

She nodded.

"So I tell you I love you, and you just say, 'Sorry, you're wrong'?"

"Harper, you're using me to work out something."

"Well, how about you, then?"

"What about me?"

"Are you falling in love with me?"

"No."

Wow.

"You mean that?"

She nodded. "I do mean that."

Shit.

"Still glad you asked?"

"But do you think you could ever fall in love with me?"

"I have no idea."

Right. "And so here's another question, then. Do you know, in any part of your heart, that this thing between us is definitely not forever?"

"Harper, why can't you just enjoy being with me?"

"Because I guess I'm not that kind of guy, finally. I wanted to be, but I'm not. And I'm not even asking if you know that we *are* forever, anyway. I'm not even asking if you *hope* we're forever. I'm just asking if you know for sure—beyond all doubt—that we are *not* forever. That this definitely will not last. It's not a complicated question."

"I have no idea how to answer. You sound like a lawyer cross-examining me."

"But 'no idea' is great. That's a great answer. Just say, 'I don't know one way or another if this is forever.' "

"Are you asking me to marry you? Because that's a bullshit way of going about it."

"I am not asking you to marry me, Joan. I'm just trying to find out if you know for sure there's a time limit to this thing."

"What if the answer's yes? What if I just *said* that: 'Yes, I do know it's not forever.' "

"I'd be gone."

"Oh, really?"

I nodded. "Yep."

"And that's your way of putting me at ease?"

"It's my way of being honest."

"For God's sake, Harper, you're a wonderful boy, we were having a wonderful time, and someday a very nice girl is going to love you to death. Come on, stop it. I can't stand seeing you so wounded and pouty. Make love to me, or something."

Joan pulled me toward her again, and began kissing me, and said, "Oh, see, this is what I kept trying to tell you! No slowing down, no trying to protect me from evil. I'm a big, strong girl, and you're not going to break anything here. It really reminds me of right after I got pregnant. Sigmund lied to me that he'd been snipped and I found out I was pregnant after I got back here to New York."

"Why are you telling me this?"

"I'm just telling you why I did what I did afterward. Because I was so angry."

"Is this why you broke up with Sigmund?"

"He was also fifty years old and I was twenty-three and I wasn't going to be trapped. But what I was trying to tell you is that I had to get the locks changed after Sigmund left, and this big Irish boy came to do the job. He was hilarious. He'd had an ear shot off by the Ulster constabulary. You know what I did? I've never told anyone. I had sex with him on the floor." She laughed at herself.

"Well, that's really wonderful."

"I just wanted you to know what you were punishing me for. I wanted you to punish me some more for it."

By what, being the working stiff Mick letting this princess

boss me around and watch television while I worked—take a shower and parade around in her towel and ask if I couldn't please hurry up? Well, fine, and here's your custom-ordered abuse all running toward some conclusion now, and I was exhilarated and also confused at finding a lifetime's objectless and unknown hatred being shaped and channeled through Joanie's physical being, as if I were trying to break her apart or thus somehow do myself some good.

When we lay still again, the room was dark and lucid with ambient city light. She said, "Wow, you know, baby, if you'd stopped saying that stuff . . ."

"What stuff?"

"At the end about 'Come, bitch, come.' "

"What about it?"

"I swear I almost had some whole other kind of orgasm." I remember the way her long hands shook as she lit a cigarette.

"A better orgasm?" I asked.

But her mind was working away again, hiding in a performance of ferocious engagement with the moment itself, the terrific and funny journey of her life as she was once again rewriting it. She said, "Exponentially better. The final *ur*-gasm, even. I think my skeleton would've melted into my pelvis. It was like right there."

"So what happened?"

Joan bit her lip and said, "You just needed to shut up."

"I thought you liked the talking."

"I do, but it distracted me." She shook her head at the missed opportunity. "I think it would've changed my life. I would've been yours forever. What were you thinking, anyway? While you were fucking me?"

I told her.

"A class-based rape fantasy! I *love* it. That's absolutely

great! You want to know what I'm thinking? I'm a girl in your class, one of your students. We're thinking the same thing."

Then, back to it, until Joan smiled—peaceful and sparkling. She said, "Okay, guess what I'm thinking now."

I ignored her, gripping disappointment like a club.

"I was thinking, like, I wanted to say, 'Daddy, what did I do so wrong for you to fuck me so hard?' Isn't that funny? Really. 'Daddy, what did I do so wrong that you have to fuck me like this?' Am I not the most *twisted* little child?" She laughed loud and high, shivering with a hilarity I found infuriating for its dismissal of the person I actually was. But along with the disappointment, I felt a new freedom from restraint, and from trying to save Joan or anyone else, from being anything but the outraged monster I'd never known until now I most truly was. And while her eyes teared up with happiness, begging big Mr. Artois to fuck her always, it was glorious for both of them, because bad Joan-Joanie knew she'd been asking for this and wanted only this—and how lucky to know what you wanted!—and she knew also that if Mr. Artois didn't beat this into her, she'd never learn, and it was better Mr. Artois than somebody else, because at least he loved her. Astonished to be here, and to have let myself get so trampled down and still not to have rejected the sad venting of all my indignance through fucking, I fought as if to find out how Joan or the idea of Joan or whatever the hell it was (the desire preceding its chimera-like object) could so relentlessly draw me in and spit me out and never, ever just melt and soften and need me and love me and forgive all my flaws and tell me I was okay and worthy.

"Cash," she was saying, "this is what I've been trying to tell you all this time. You don't have to slow down and try to protect me from evil." So I said that I just couldn't satisfy this terribly naughty little student of mine, could I? Because as big and powerful as I could imagine myself to be while I spanked her and told her what a marvelous white ass she had, I also told her that I knew she'd prefer Gujie's masterful Frenchman, too, and she said, Yes, of course, so I asked if she wouldn't also prefer Bernie's handsome American and Sigmund's freezer-cured Bratwurst—Absolutely! her face said—and did she not need her mean old mother and Eliza and all the others watching? Yes, her eyes confessed, she did indeed have a truly bottomless need, but back came the news that, unfortunately, she only had bad old Harper tonight, and so when Joan reached to pull off the condom—as she always did—Harp finally thought, *Okay, the hell with you, I'm done. Take responsibility for your own life.*

She spun around in horror.

"Wait, you didn't come inside me, did you?"

I nodded.

"What?"

"You pulled off the condom, Joan."

Stepping into the bathroom, she said, "What would you do if I got pregnant?"

"Joan, you're kidding, right?"

"I'm afraid I'm not kidding."

"You're menstruating. Your chances of getting pregnant are almost nil."

"What would you *want* me to do if I got pregnant?"

"No way." I started dressing as fast as I could. "I'm not playing this game."

"Answer the question."

"Sorry, not in the mood." I had my shoes on now, my belt. I was reaching for my wallet.

"My oh my, are you an asshole. How can you . . ."

"It's ridiculous. You're being ridiculous." I shoved the last few things into my shoulder bag while Joan, who was better at all-out warfare than I, threw her heart into a final, farewell volley of viciousness, about how she'd always ordered me not to expect anything, and that I'd ignored her because it wasn't what I wanted, and now I'd ejaculated inside her against her will like some kind of fucking rapist, and told her to get rid of the baby, like on some perverse after-school special, and it all proved that even if she *were* in the right space to love somebody new, which she absolutely was not, it would absolutely never be me, because she needed a man who was competent enough to care for her in a strong and adult manner. "You think everything I do is a referendum on you," she screamed. "And it's not! It's about how scared I am of my own life! But all that's a mystery to you, no matter how many times I tell you, because your mother has you paralyzed with her bullshit about how you're so sexy and perfect that you genuinely cannot believe a woman when she says, 'I don't love you.' She's got you living in this fantasy universe of family mythologies, with your father as the freedom fighter who can't quite satisfy her, and she's Marilyn Monroe and you're her valiant back-door man, young Prince Harper needing his own wounded upper-class princess to restore Mommy to her lost station in life. But you can't get up the guts to just cut the self-pity and be a man. Not your mother's childish notion of it, either, or your father's, but your own. And now it's all ruined between us, all our sweetness is turned to shit."

As I opened her door, ready to walk out of it, I did my very best in return. "But how did you want me to answer the question, anyway, Joan? Did you want me to say you should keep the baby and we'll raise it together, so you could remind me how little money I have and how you'd never waste your life with a chump like me? Or do you want me to tell you to get an abortion? Maybe that's it. Maybe that's the one that would really confirm whatever you think about me. You could add me to the list of evildoers who've ruined your life. Your mother, your father, your boss, and your boss's boss, and me. Poor little Joanie, always getting involved with such terrible humans. But you know the truth? You're a manipulative, materialistic infant with a mile-wide mean streak. And that's fine, because I'm over this. I'm done. Okay? So, here: I would want you to get an abortion, Joan. You happy?"

Or something like that. And when I was done, and Joan was crying for the first time since we'd met, I got a taxi to the airport.

The noon white guys scrambled on a People's Park pickup court—yells at the free throw, seagulls scavenging, and a familiar homeless man, a decades-old regular of Telegraph, sat beside me and filled the air with the smell of the piss and shit in which he lived. I started to my feet, and his small brown eyes met mine with a glimmer of recognition. Fifteen years before, I'd paid this guy a dollar to tape a piece of string to a quarter, go into the Silver Ball arcade, drop that quarter into the slot of the Missile Command video game, and pull it up and down a hundred times on the machine's internal game credit button. Maybe half a dozen times, since I was twelve years old, we'd made this same deal—one dollar, a hundred games. Then I could smoke hash in the bushes, head inside, and fail to save the world from nuclear annihilation for a couple of hours; rail-thin and feeling very adult and proud for being on that street at all, as if it were the great, wide world. And here this guy was, with his matted hair and Thorazine eyes, decades past whatever irremediable tragedy had befallen him, still muttering his self-justifying insanity, still wearing a shit-stained overcoat and sole-less sneakers, feet black as ever. I'd avoided pulling that string-taped-to-the-quarter trick myself because I'd heard the Silver Ball employees were into vigilante justice, and sure enough, after doing my dirty work for a few weeks, this poor lost heart had been caught, taken into an alley behind the arcade, and savagely beaten—nose smashed, tooth broken on the pavement, rib cracked, picked up by the city's Human Services van.

"Get an abortion."

That's what I'd said to Joan. Me. A guy who once considered himself a paragon of sensitivity. And the screwy part was that I'd felt great saying it. I'd intended to hurt, and I'd succeeded. I'd thought about this all day on the plane home—I'd managed a standby on a discount carrier that next afternoon—and I'd thought about it the next day, too. Walking toward the upscale boutiques of College Avenue, experimenting with relief—with the possibility that I'd gotten out alive and wouldn't even be crushed at the end—I wondered if I'd been trying to make Joan say such things from the start. Maybe that had been the point. Maybe I'd wanted somebody to shove it all in my face, so I could take a good look. Mom this, Dad that, me the other thing, yada-yada. It was all more or less true, I really did need to get over it, and yet it was also true that I was far too prone to damning myself to live with a woman who encouraged me in that way. Even if she really was the most exciting person I'd ever met. Even if there really was something about her that seemed magically formed as a physical and emotional counterpart to myself. Because she did seem that way. I could spend my whole life with this woman, I found myself thinking, and always be attracted to her and always be spellbound by whatever came out of her mouth. But it didn't matter, because the real incorrigibility in me—in addition to the emotional immaturity and the mother dependency and the calculating narcissism—was the navel-gazer's capacity for self-obsession, and especially for whirlpools of self-criticism, the certainty that everything about me was wrong and had to change. So I'd be a fool to staple myself to a woman who fended off her own misery by nuking everyone around her.

At a sidewalk table, I let my thoughts wander to the boom-time buzz of the pedestrian crowds, and to the Audi TT and Mercedes Kompressor convertibles, the hip little shops teeming with shoppers. America, as far as I could tell, had more money than it knew what to do with. But not everybody: approaching me with a stroller was an unbearably lovely woman in white painter paints and a white long-sleeve T-shirt and work boots. Her choppy short hair had originally been brown, but peroxide flecking gave it the sexy affect of a bookish introvert wryly staying abreast of fashion because she liked boys and knew you had to make a move or two if you wanted to date. Her features were the very picture of earnest intelligence, and in those clear brown eyes I imagined that I saw irony, humor, and kindness. On her lips lay the hint of a smirk, and about what? About the pathetic line tried by the enviro nonprofit guy in line at the bagel stand, whom she'd found a little sweet?

I headed to campus next, to collect my mail, and found Shauna alone in her undecorated office, frizzy hair in a bun and her wide-set eyes forgiving and friendly. She wore a long burgundy skirt with her boots and a white turtleneck. She looked great, and determined not to be hurt. "I was in Marin yesterday," she said, her voice cooled by the too many days since we'd spoken. "The wild mustard was blooming. I looked for radish blossoms, too, but then I remembered what you said, about how they don't come until April. But the grasses were all green and the poppies were out, and the oxalis and alyssum. You would've been in heaven."

She was so smart and gentle, and she liked me fine. And she was going to be a professor.

"Utterly in heaven. I got happy just picturing you."

I smiled.

"It's nice to see your face, Harper."

"It's great to see yours."

"I miss you."

"How's the job thing going?"

"N.Y.U. doesn't want me, but I'm down to the last two at Amherst. I'm giving a talk next week." She nodded, sucked in a breath and held it there. "Well, it was great to see you, Harp."

"Yeah, great to see you, too, Shauna."

"Yeah."

"Well."

"Hmm?"

"What?"

"Oh, I thought you were going to say something."

"Oh, no."

"I better go."

"Oh, okay."

"Bye."

"Bye, girl."

"Hey, Harp?"

"Yeah?"

"Nothing."

"You sure?"

"Yeah. See you around, huh?"

"Look, I promised myself, the moment I saw you, that I wouldn't do this, but my parents are giving a little party for me tonight, at Pasand. I'd love it if you came."

I showed up alone at the Thai barbecue place from our first date and found Shauna's new father to be a perfectly urbane Manhattan orthopedist, and not so bad-looking after all. A few of Shauna's and my colleagues were there, too, eating those baby back ribs—earnestly devoted to a vision of themselves as "culture workers," changing the world by changing freshman-comp reading lists. I barely spoke to Shauna—she was the belle of the ball and wary of me—but afterward, inside her cottage, I felt accused by Shauna's little gods and goddesses, and her stacks of books, the futon couch, the ladder leading up to the "cloud." She got out the Scotch, and as I reached for ice, I saw those same old notes, clips, and photographs on the refrigerator—Bert and Ernie, *Vegetarians Taste Better.* On the futon, I neither waited nor asked, just kissed her and felt a welling hurry to heal myself with her warmth.

"Cowboy!"

"Yeah, baby."

"So rough." She looked into my eyes, alert. Then she said, "Whatever you've been doing when you're not with me—and I don't want to know what it is—you're not quite done."

And she was almost right, because I did answer the phone as I drove home across the Bay Bridge, through the glittering light.

"Hey, baby," Joan said, calling from New York, as if nothing had happened.

"What's up?"

"I saw my mother today."

"For your birthday?"

"It was sad," Joan said, "because we both realized how little she knew about my life. And I told her a fair amount, like this disappointment I had trying to get into Juilliard and my trouble at work, and I could tell she was happy to know but also really sad she hadn't been there to help. And part of me wanted to come out and say, 'Goddamn it, Mom, when have you *ever* helped?' She had this incredible present for me, too, a gorgeous Tiffany pendant of a butterfly, with diamond eyes and ruby wings. I'm not even going to tell you how much that thing must have cost. She tried to say nice things, like that she knew how it hurt to lose a career, and to worry about making a worthwhile life, but I started to feel like, 'Okay, come on. I've done my part here, I've been the good daughter, let's cut to the chase.' And I could see my mom's eyes sort of bouncing around the table, and she kept flipping this bit of cake with her fork. She gets so choked up, and she sort of beat around the bush trying to tell me how hard her life had been and how sorry she was about the way I'd grown up. And then she said her big thing. She said, 'Joanie, after your father left, it's like there was a black hole in my heart that made it impossible for me to love you.' " Joan stopped, as if to let this sink in. As if to let it affect me somehow. "And see, nobody's believed me all these years when I said my mother did not love me. So I guess I'm not exactly feeling buoyed." Mrs. Artois hadn't included a necklace with the pendant. "So the gift was incomplete," Joan said, "which they always are from her. And after lunch we stopped in this jewelry shop and I hung the pendant on a chain around my neck, and she looked at it and said, 'Oh yes, that *is* lovely. But it's too expensive for today.' And that was it. We've had our first birthday lunch in ages, she's come all the way to New York and given me her big present, she's said her big, difficult thing, and she can't close the deal. So they put away the chain and we walked out and stood on the sidewalk, and we sort of *waved* good-bye."

"That's an awful story, Joan."

"Where are you?"

"On the Bay Bridge."

"So late at night."

"Yeah."

"Seeing somebody?"

"Joan, you're like emotional heroin to me. Do you know that?"

"What an ugly thing to say."

"But I mean it. It's yummy, but not nourishing."

"But don't you want to give it a try? Things have just been

so much worse in my life than you know, Harper, and I've been so afraid of showing you."

"Why afraid?"

"People don't love me when they find out who I really am."

I had a weakness for such talk.

"And that's why I put you through all those tests."

"Really?"

"I've had this sort of ugly thing inside for my entire life, and I'm always afraid of letting people see it, or of even looking at it myself, so I fill up my life with bullshit, with sex and toys and whatever, and try to keep moving. But for the first time, I guess I'm getting a glimpse of what it would be like to feel good in my skin. And I feel like my sanity was so stormy and precarious in California, and your love was this very delicate teacup balanced on a fragile saucer, and so sweet and full, and I had to carry it so far, and I was so tired that I worried I'd drop it and feel awful again. I'd ruin it like I always do. So I went ahead and ruined it anyway, to kill the suspense."

"And?"

"You just touched me so well and so tenderly. I want us to have that touching again."

I did, too.

"God, if only I could make you believe me."

"I believe you. But here's the thing, okay? I don't know if I'm actually strong enough for you. I'm too porous, or something. I can't take all the bad language and the lies and the fights and reunions, and on and on and on. I just want to date somebody, like a normal human being, and come home in the evening and have her say, 'Oh hi, sweetie, how was your day?' and have her actually want to hear my reply. Because you have never once done that. Not since the day we met."

"Is that true?"

"Not once. You have never, not a single time, not even just now, have you asked how I'm doing. Just the simple, polite 'Hey, how was your day?' Never. And I can't be called a pussy anymore. Or a momma's boy. It's crazy."

"Okay, see, but I think that's exactly what I want, too. If only I could make you understand." She breathed hard and I heard the phone shuffle. She said, "I feel like that guy from INXS—that Australian rock star—who died in the middle of his autoerotic asphyxiation, like hanging himself from the showerhead while he was jacking off so his head feels like it's going to explode, and then you just come like you gave birth."

I laughed out loud. She was certainly an original. "That's supposed to be comforting?"

"But it's so true! Oh, I wish you'd believe me."

"I should probably get off the phone, okay?"

"I thought you were falling in love with me. Where did that go so fast? In one stupid fight?"

"I *was* falling in love with you. I'm still in love with you. But I'm not going to do it."

"Wait, okay. Okay. But there is one more thing you should know."

I waited.

"Something I was just too scared to say."

Yes?

"I love you, Harp."

Oh no.

"And I don't speak those words lightly."

Oh no.

"I really do, baby. I love you."

And for most of the time I've been telling this story, I've wanted to end here: at the place where Joan finally says she loves me and I walk away. That's my big chance to say that I came out on top, despite all the humiliation. But in the telling, which I've done far too much of, my love affair with Joan has become a kind of crystal ball for me. Every time I look inside, it looks different, and I mostly just see whatever's on my own mind now, this week. Every time I decide I need to rethink the whole narrative from scratch and tell it from a whole new point of view. And yet it never helps; the story never stops moving around. So maybe I'll try ending here instead: before I got off the phone that night, and before I drove back to my apartment at Ocean Beach, I said, "I don't want to make a real go of it, Joan. I really don't. But I also do love you, and there's a chance I always will."

ACKNOWLEDGMENTS

For their patience, forbearance, and most of all their insight, I am forever grateful to Ethan Nosowsky, John Glusman, and Diana Finch. Doug Armstrong, Thomas Farber, and Apollinaire Scherr also read various drafts, and did their best to save me from myself. Nancy Harrow kept me from blundering certain details, as did Aaron Davidman and Deborah Fink. Anton Krukowski was an especially devoted and supportive reader, mastering the role of the writer's perfect friend.

A NOTE ABOUT THE AUTHOR

Daniel Duane is the author of four previous books, including the memoir *Caught Inside: A Surfer's Year on the California Coast* (North Point Press, 1996). He has written for *The New York Times Magazine*, *GQ*, *Men's Journal*, *Esquire*, and *Outside*, among other publications, and he lives in San Francisco with his daughter, Hannah, and his wife, the writer Elizabeth Weil.